STAR WARS

THE EMPIRE STRIKES BACK

™

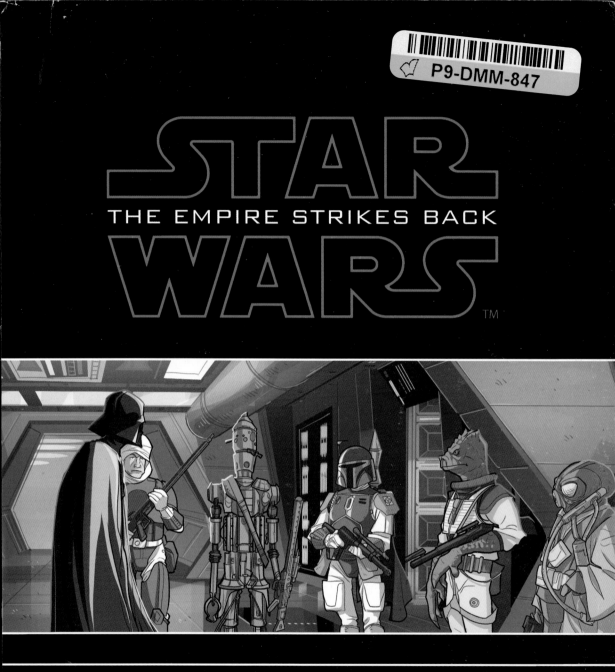

A LONG TIME AGO, IN A GALAXY FAR, FAR AWAY....

2

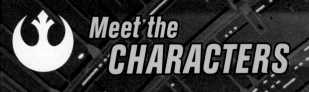

Meet the CHARACTERS

LUKE SKYWALKER

Luke Skywalker was just a farmer with the dream of becoming a pilot. Now he has become a **rebel leader** and a skillful **X-wing commander**. Since his Jedi Master Obi-Wan Kenobi was killed by Darth Vader, his Force abilities remained undeveloped.

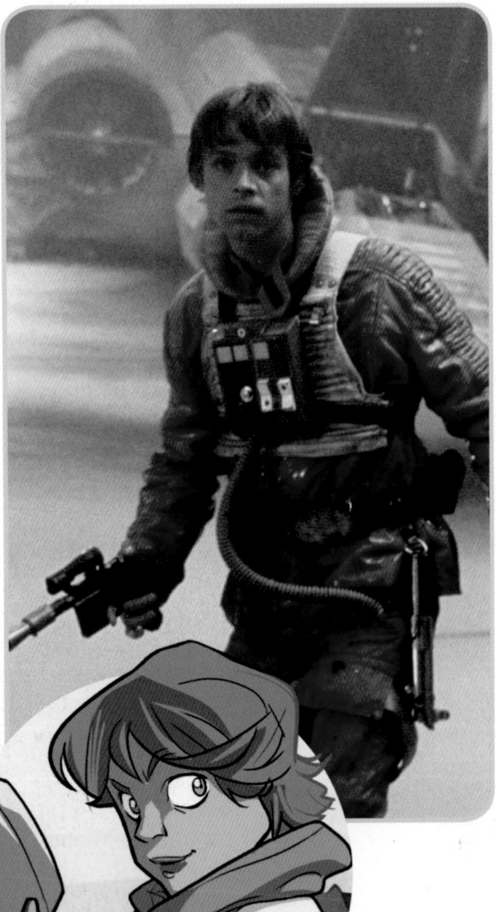

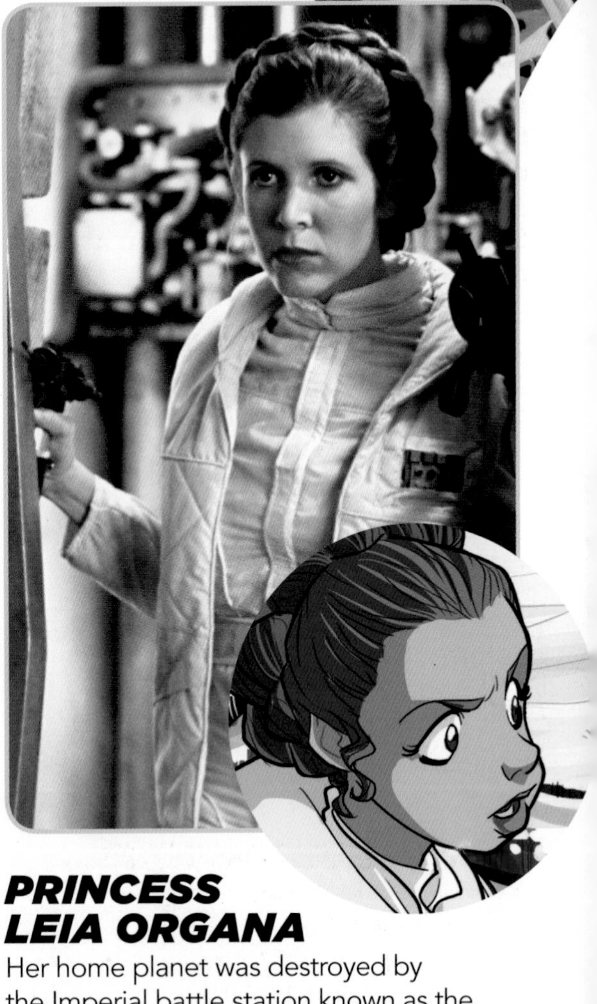

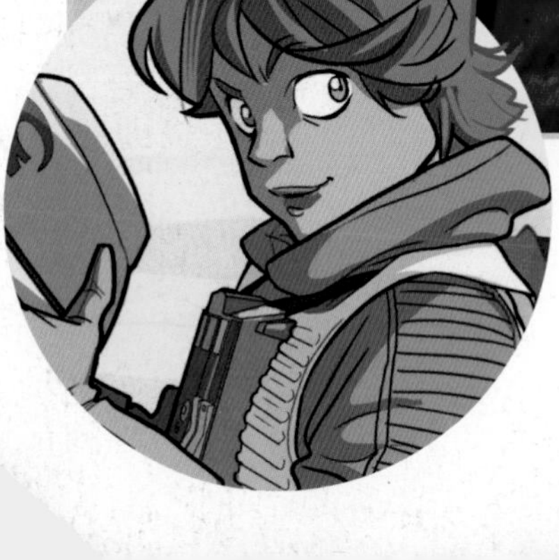

PRINCESS LEIA ORGANA

Her home planet was destroyed by the Imperial battle station known as the **Death Star**. Exposed as a rebel, Princess Leia is no longer a diplomat, but a full-time **leader** of the Rebel Alliance.

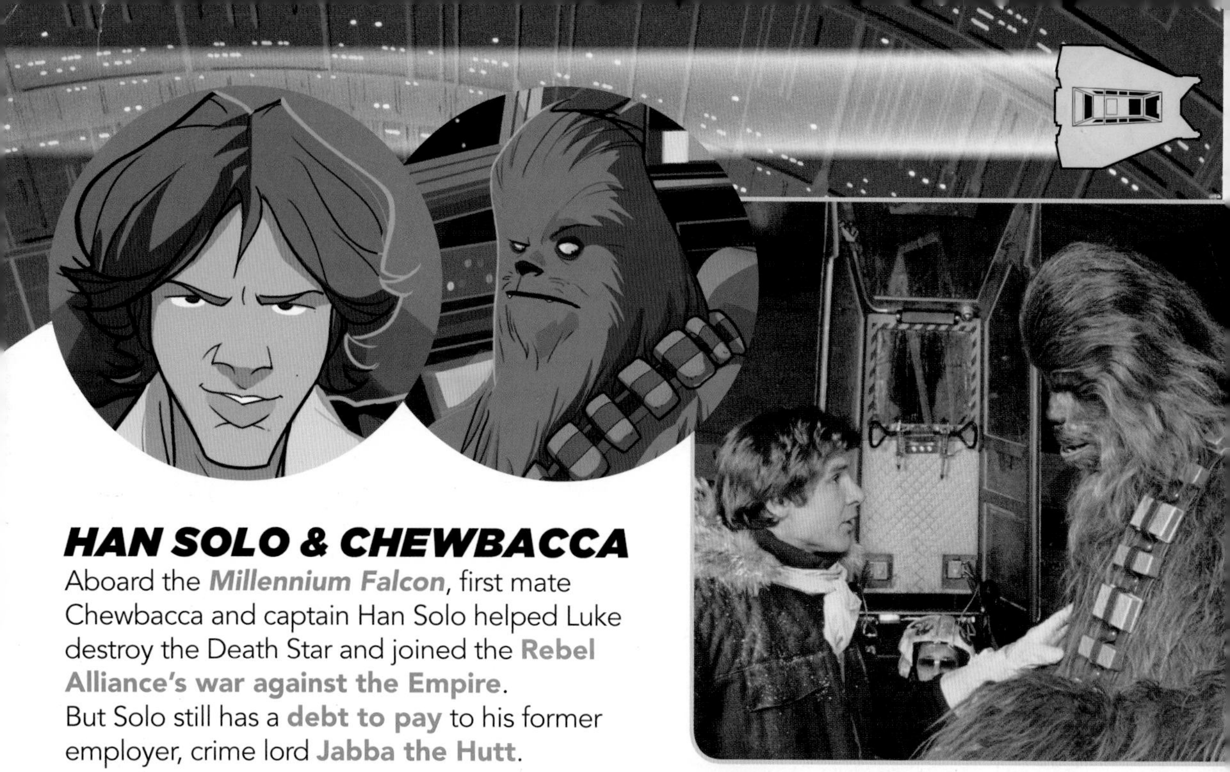

HAN SOLO & CHEWBACCA

Aboard the **Millennium Falcon**, first mate Chewbacca and captain Han Solo helped Luke destroy the Death Star and joined the **Rebel Alliance's war against the Empire**. But Solo still has a **debt to pay** to his former employer, crime lord **Jabba the Hutt**.

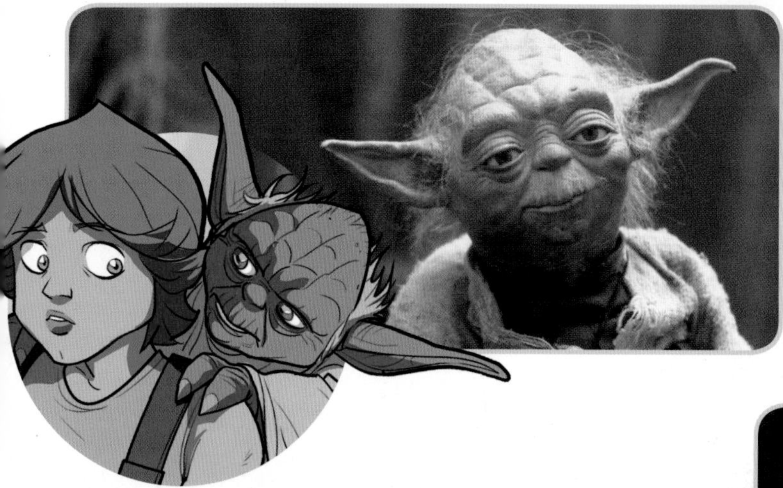

YODA

He was one of the most powerful members of the **Jedi High Council**, long before the **Clone Wars** and the rise of the Empire. Now 900 years old, Yoda lives in hiding on the remote planet **Dagobah**.

LANDO CALRISSIAN

A former smuggler, Lando was the captain of the *Millennium Falcon*. Then he lost it to his friend Han Solo in a **sabacc match**. He later won control of **Cloud City**, a gas mining outpost above the planet **Bespin**.

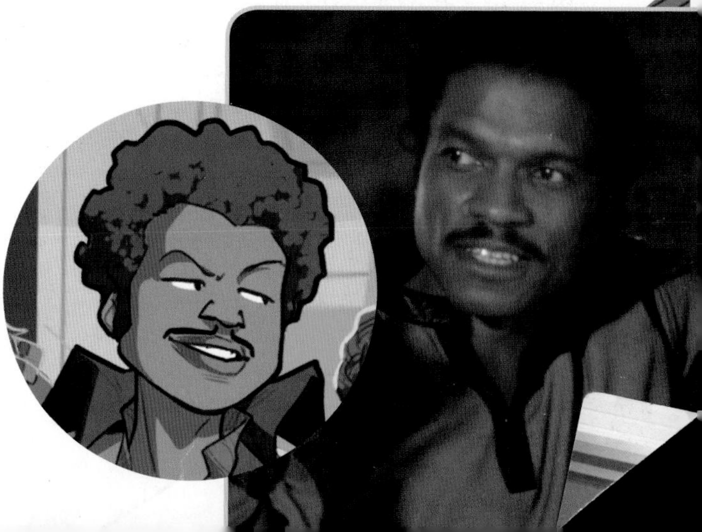

Meet the CHARACTERS

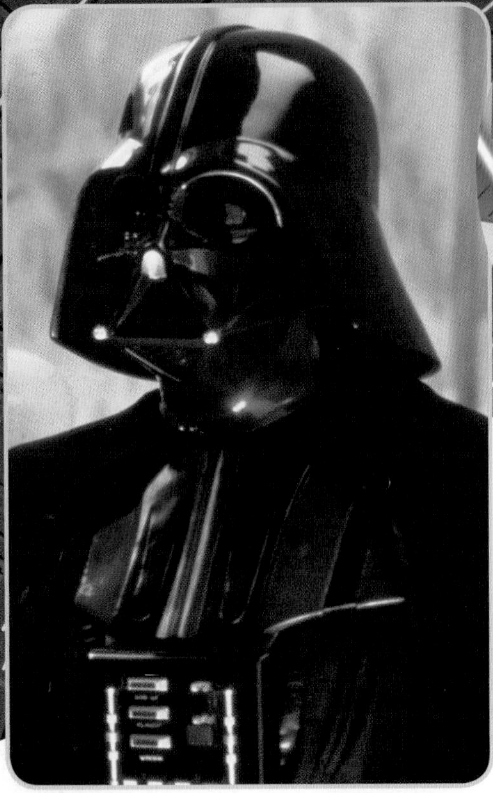

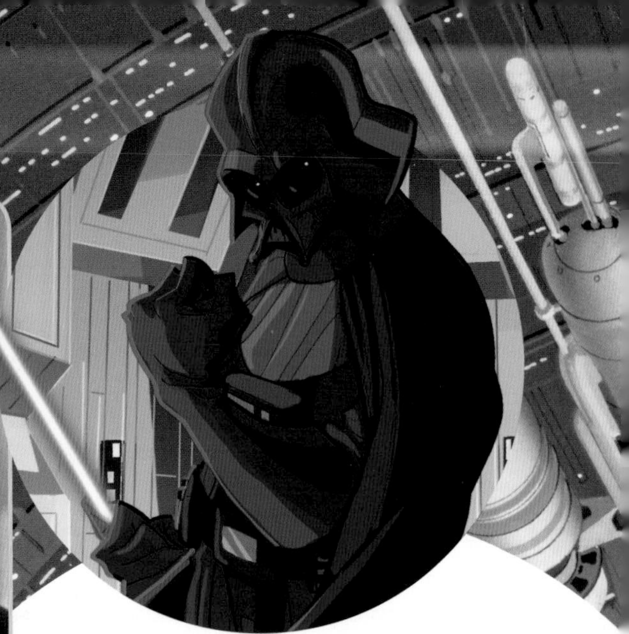

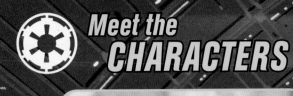

DARTH VADER

During the attack on the **Death Star**, Vader sensed a **strong Force ability** in a pilot. After Vader survived the battle station's explosion, he found out the pilot's name is **Luke Skywalker**. He is now looking for him, planning to turn him to the **dark side**.

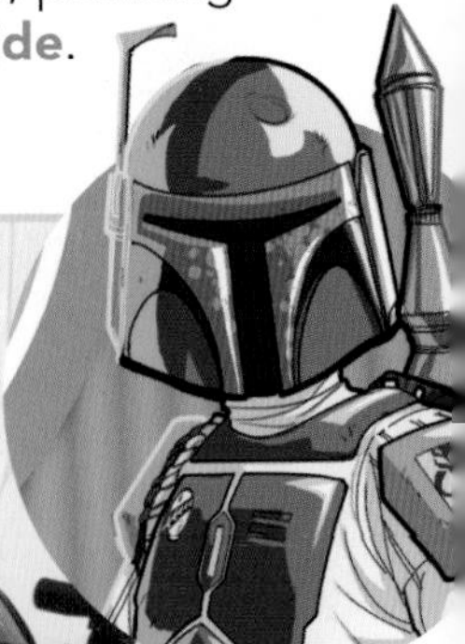

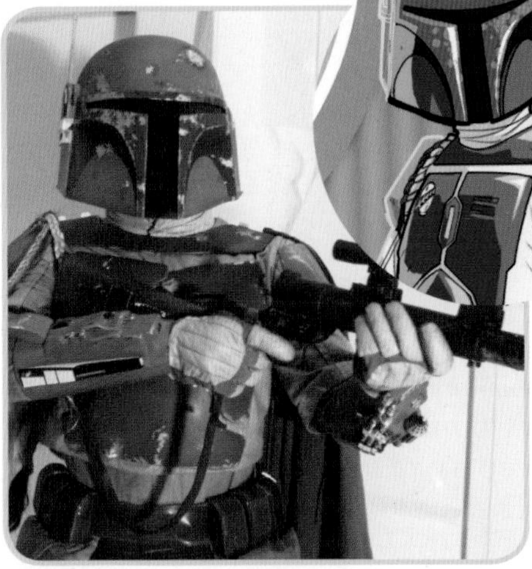

BOUNTY HUNTERS

Vile, **dangerous** and **always ready to kill**, the bounty hunters work for the highest bidder. They can be paid by crime lords to retrieve traitors as well as by Imperial commanders to track down and capture conspirators and fugitives.

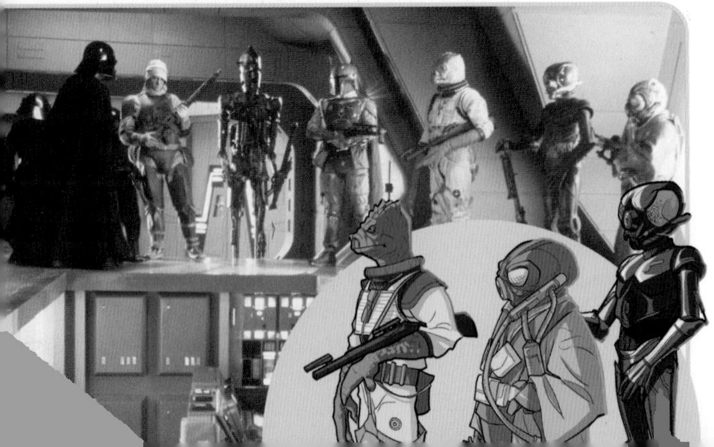

BOBA FETT

Clever, **determined** and **ruthless**, Boba Fett is considered to be the **best bounty hunter in the galaxy**.

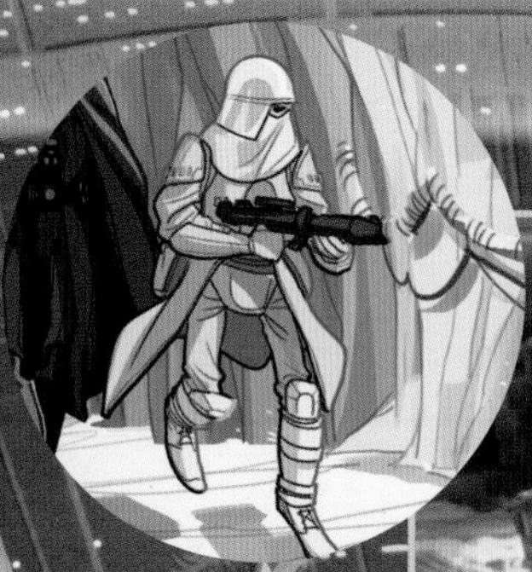

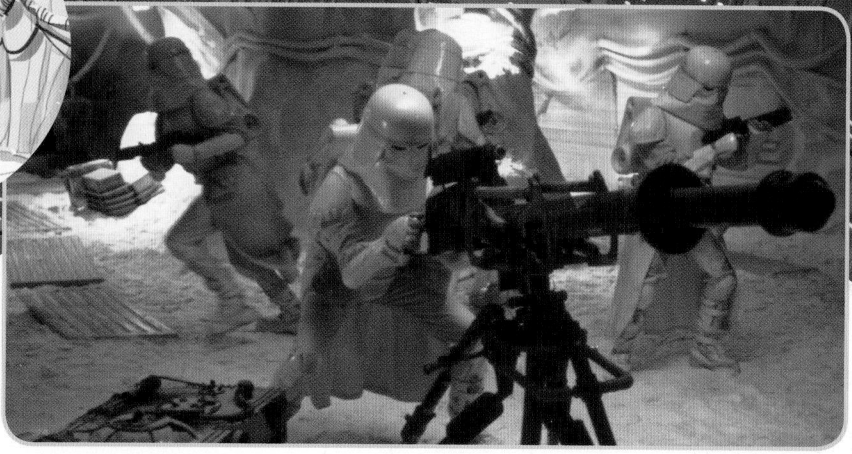

SNOWTROOPERS

Snowtroopers are specialized Imperial soldiers: thanks to their **backpacks** and suit systems they can survive extremely **low temperatures** and stay warm while they fight on ice-covered grounds.

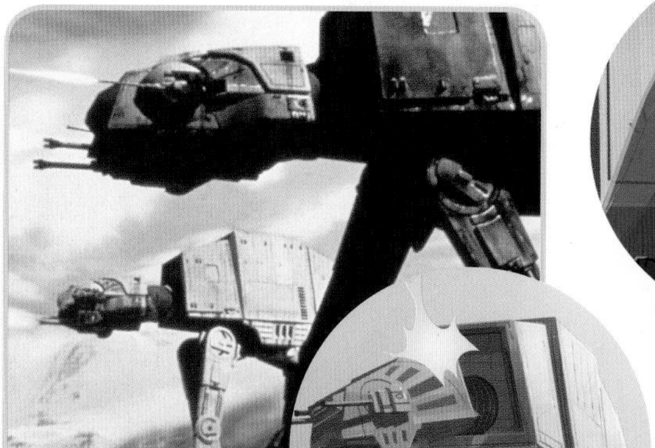

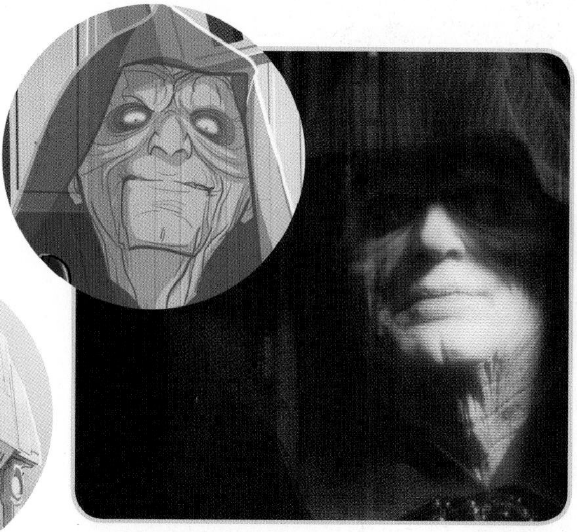

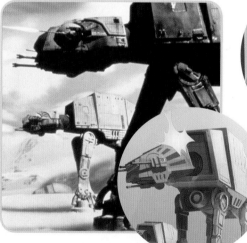

AT-AT

Massive and terrifying machines, the AT-AT (All Terrain Armor Transport) are believed to be **invincible combat units**. Shielded in almost invulnerable armor, they are equipped with heavy **laser cannons** and can carry **assault troops** inside their bodies.

EMPEROR PALPATINE

Once senator of the Republic, Emperor Palpatine is now the most feared supreme ruler of the Galaxy. He is also a **Sith Lord** and Darth Vader is his apprentice: he knows well how strong the Force is with Luke and he **doesn't want him to become a Jedi**.

Episode V
THE EMPIRE STRIKES BACK

It is a dark time for the
Rebellion. Although the Death
Star has been destroyed,
Imperial troops have driven the
Rebel forces from their hidden
base and pursued them across
the galaxy.

Evading the dreaded Imperial
Starfleet, a group of freedom
fighters led by Luke Skywalker
has established a new secret
base on the remote ice world
of Hoth.

The evil lord Darth Vader,
obsessed with finding young
Skywalker, has dispatched
thousands of remote probes into
the far reaches of space.....

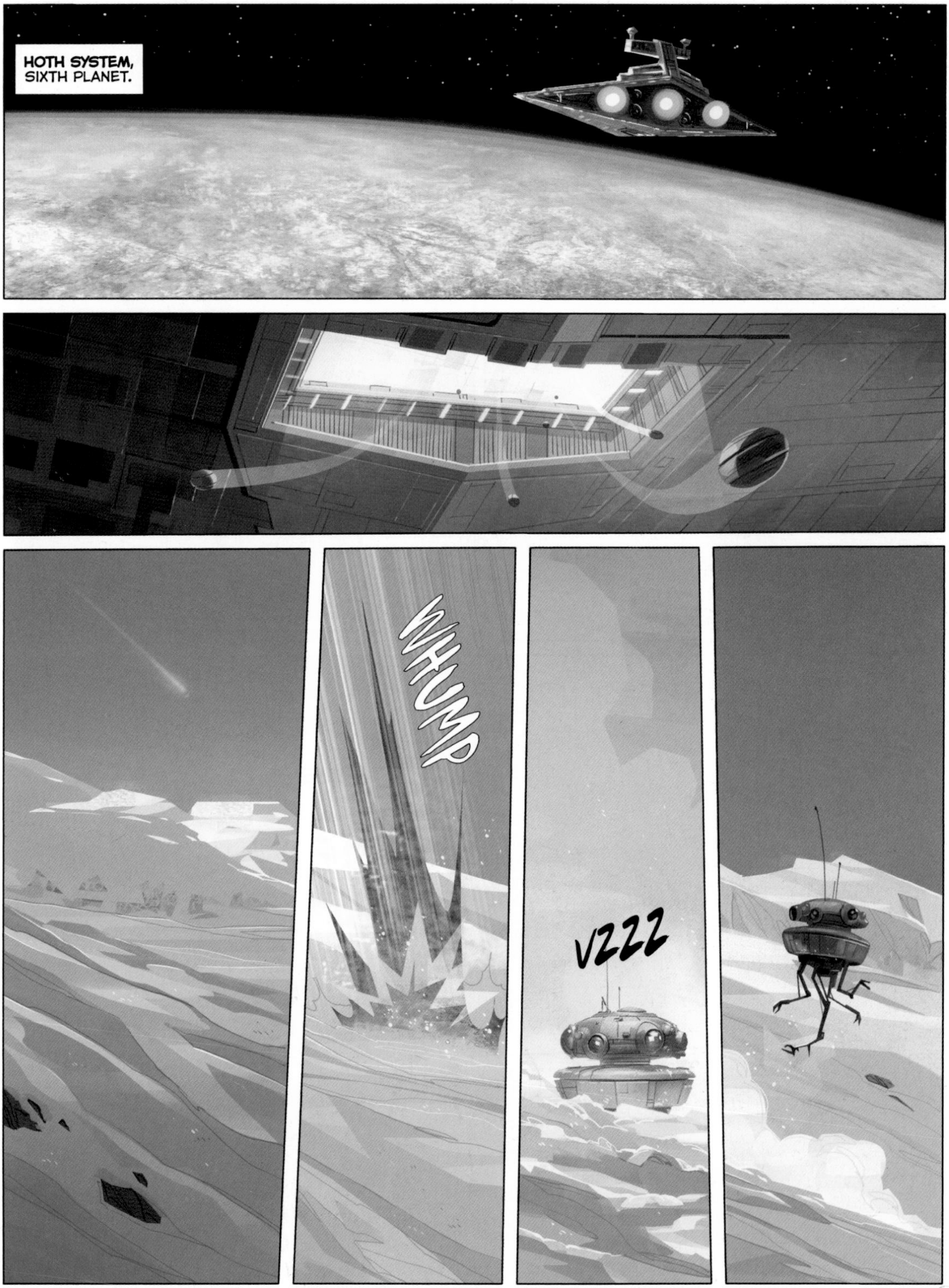
HOTH SYSTEM,
SIXTH PLANET.
WHUMP
VZZZ

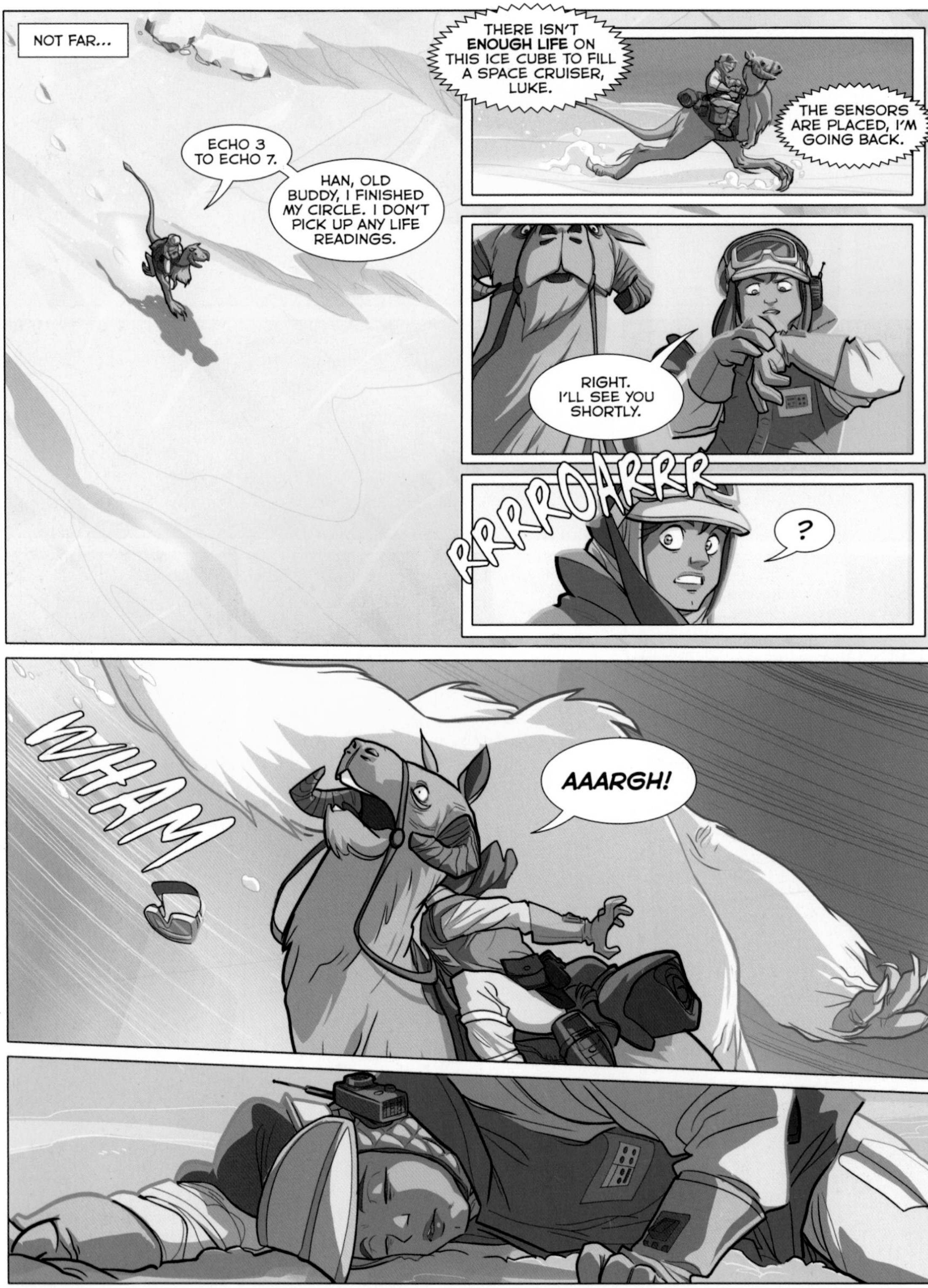
NOT FAR...
ECHO 3 TO ECHO 7.
HAN, OLD BUDDY, I FINISHED MY CIRCLE. I DON'T PICK UP ANY LIFE READINGS.
THERE ISN'T **ENOUGH LIFE** ON THIS ICE CUBE TO FILL A SPACE CRUISER, LUKE.
THE SENSORS ARE PLACED, I'M GOING BACK.
RIGHT. I'LL SEE YOU SHORTLY.
RRRROARRR
?
WHAM
AAARGH!

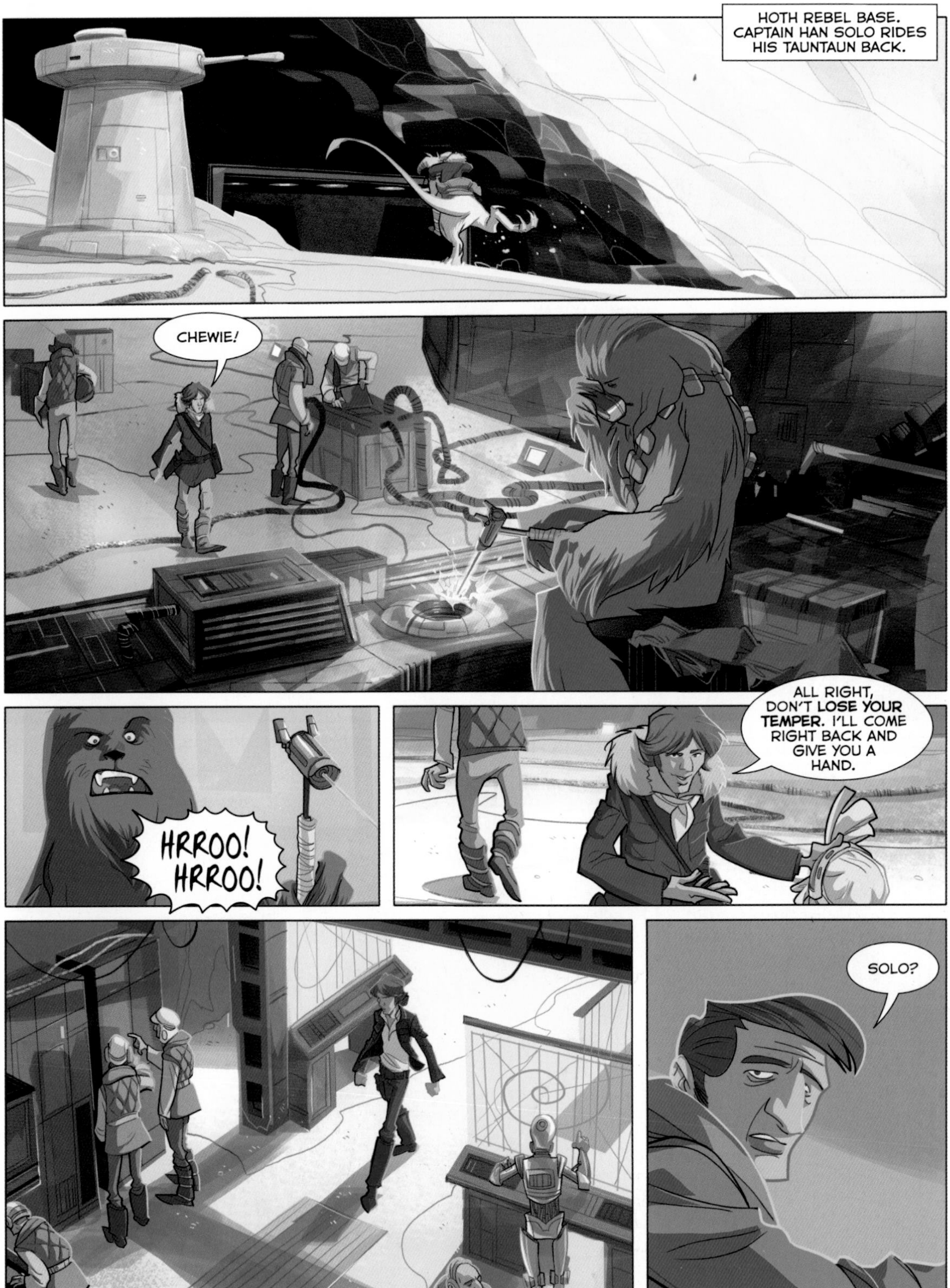
HOTH REBEL BASE. CAPTAIN HAN SOLO RIDES HIS TAUNTAUN BACK.
CHEWIE!
HRROO! HRROO!
ALL RIGHT, DON'T **LOSE YOUR TEMPER.** I'LL COME RIGHT BACK AND GIVE YOU A HAND.
SOLO?

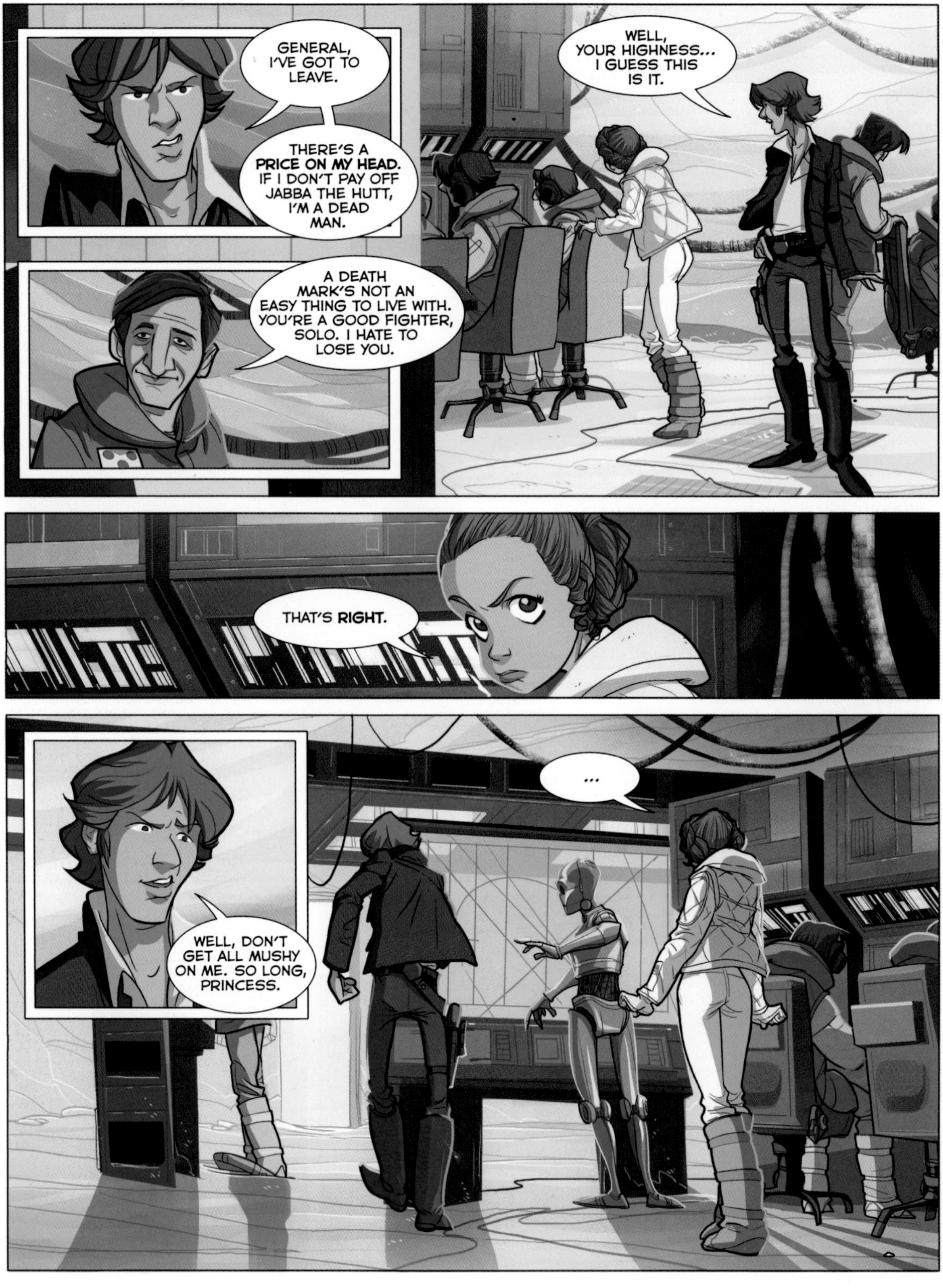

GENERAL, I'VE GOT TO LEAVE.
THERE'S A **PRICE ON MY HEAD.** IF I DON'T PAY OFF JABBA THE HUTT, I'M A DEAD MAN.
A DEATH MARK'S NOT AN EASY THING TO LIVE WITH. YOU'RE A GOOD FIGHTER, SOLO. I HATE TO LOSE YOU.
WELL, YOUR HIGHNESS... I GUESS THIS IS IT.
THAT'S **RIGHT.**
WELL, DON'T GET ALL MUSHY ON ME. SO LONG, PRINCESS.
...

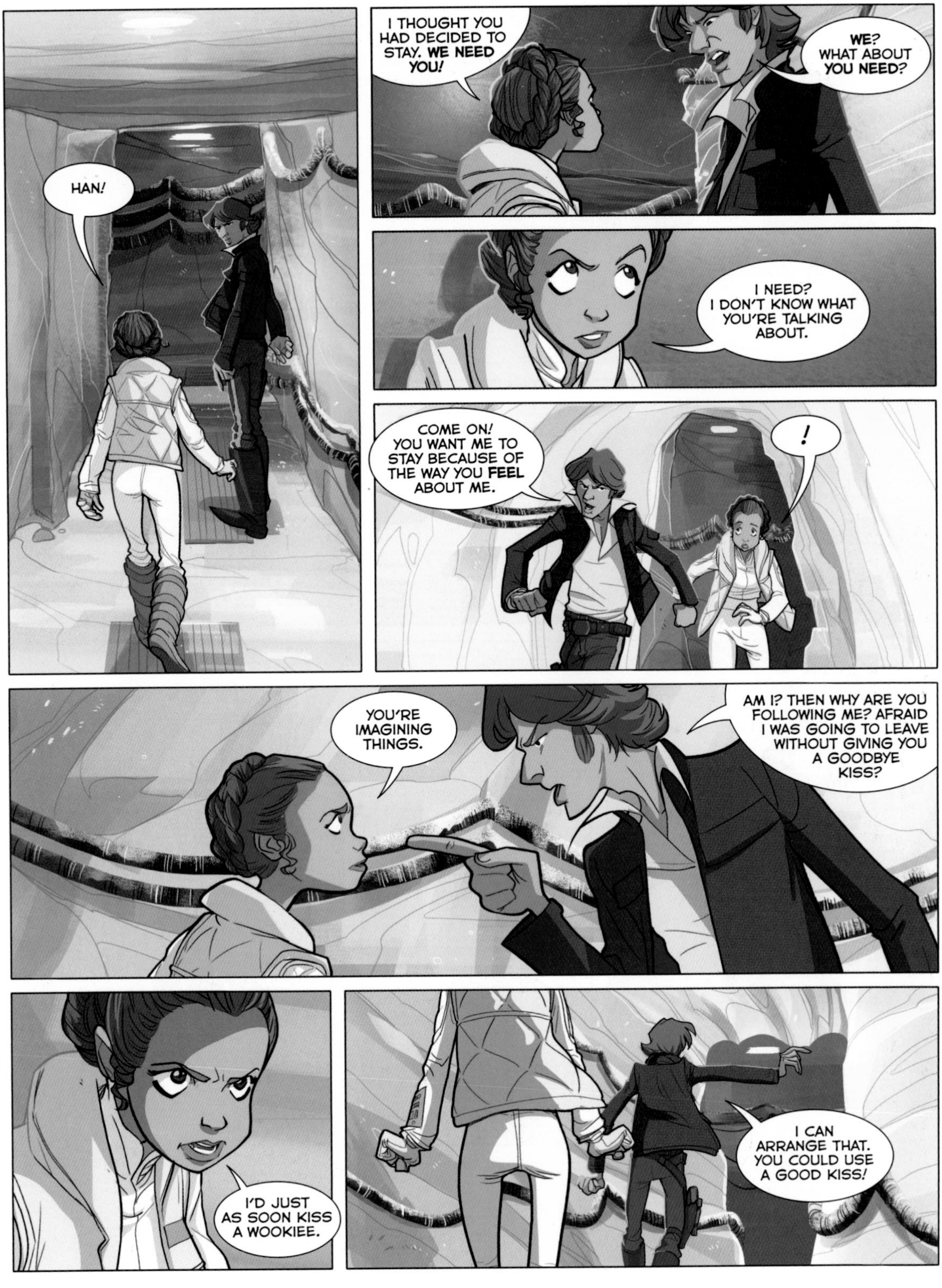
HAN!
I THOUGHT YOU HAD DECIDED TO STAY. WE NEED YOU!
WE? WHAT ABOUT YOU NEED?
I NEED? I DON'T KNOW WHAT YOU'RE TALKING ABOUT.
COME ON! YOU WANT ME TO STAY BECAUSE OF THE WAY YOU FEEL ABOUT ME.
!
YOU'RE IMAGINING THINGS.
AM I? THEN WHY ARE YOU FOLLOWING ME? AFRAID I WAS GOING TO LEAVE WITHOUT GIVING YOU A GOODBYE KISS?
I'D JUST AS SOON KISS A WOOKIEE.
I CAN ARRANGE THAT. YOU COULD USE A GOOD KISS!

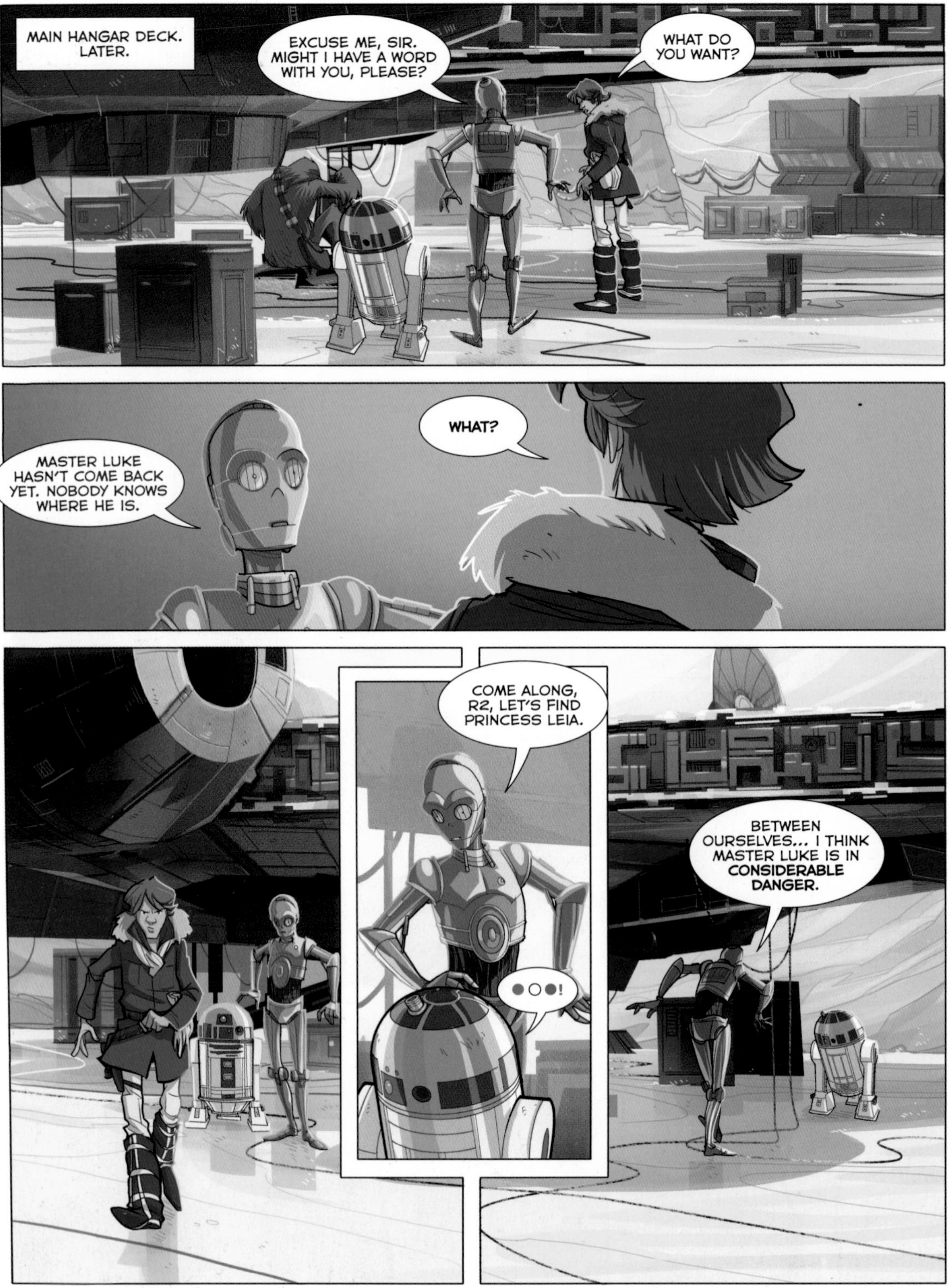
MAIN HANGAR DECK. LATER.
EXCUSE ME, SIR. MIGHT I HAVE A WORD WITH YOU, PLEASE?
WHAT DO YOU WANT?
MASTER LUKE HASN'T COME BACK YET. NOBODY KNOWS WHERE HE IS.
WHAT?
COME ALONG, R2, LET'S FIND PRINCESS LEIA.
●○●!
BETWEEN OURSELVES... I THINK MASTER LUKE IS IN **CONSIDERABLE DANGER.**

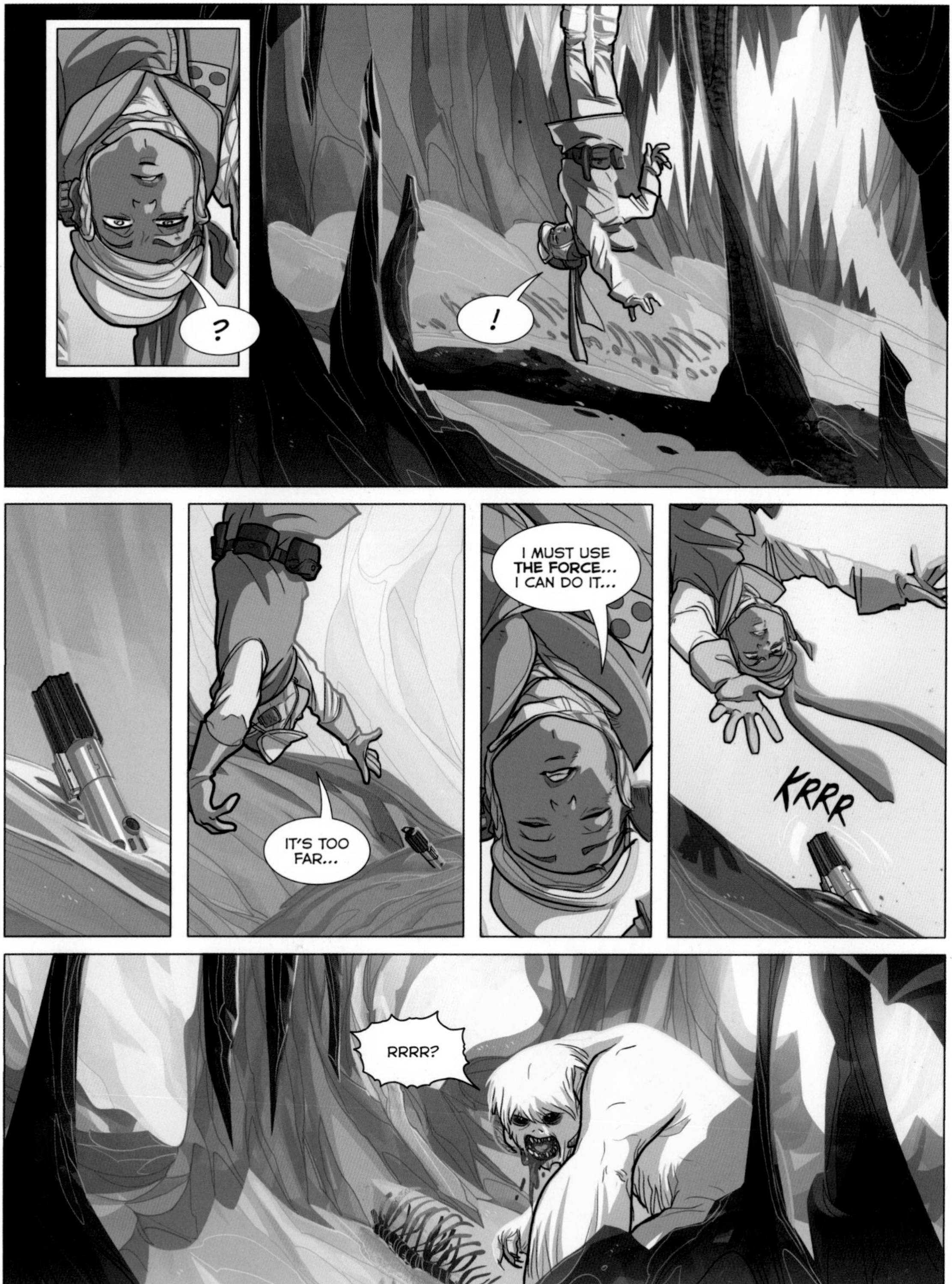
?
!
IT'S TOO FAR...
I MUST USE THE FORCE... I CAN DO IT...
KRRR
RRRR?

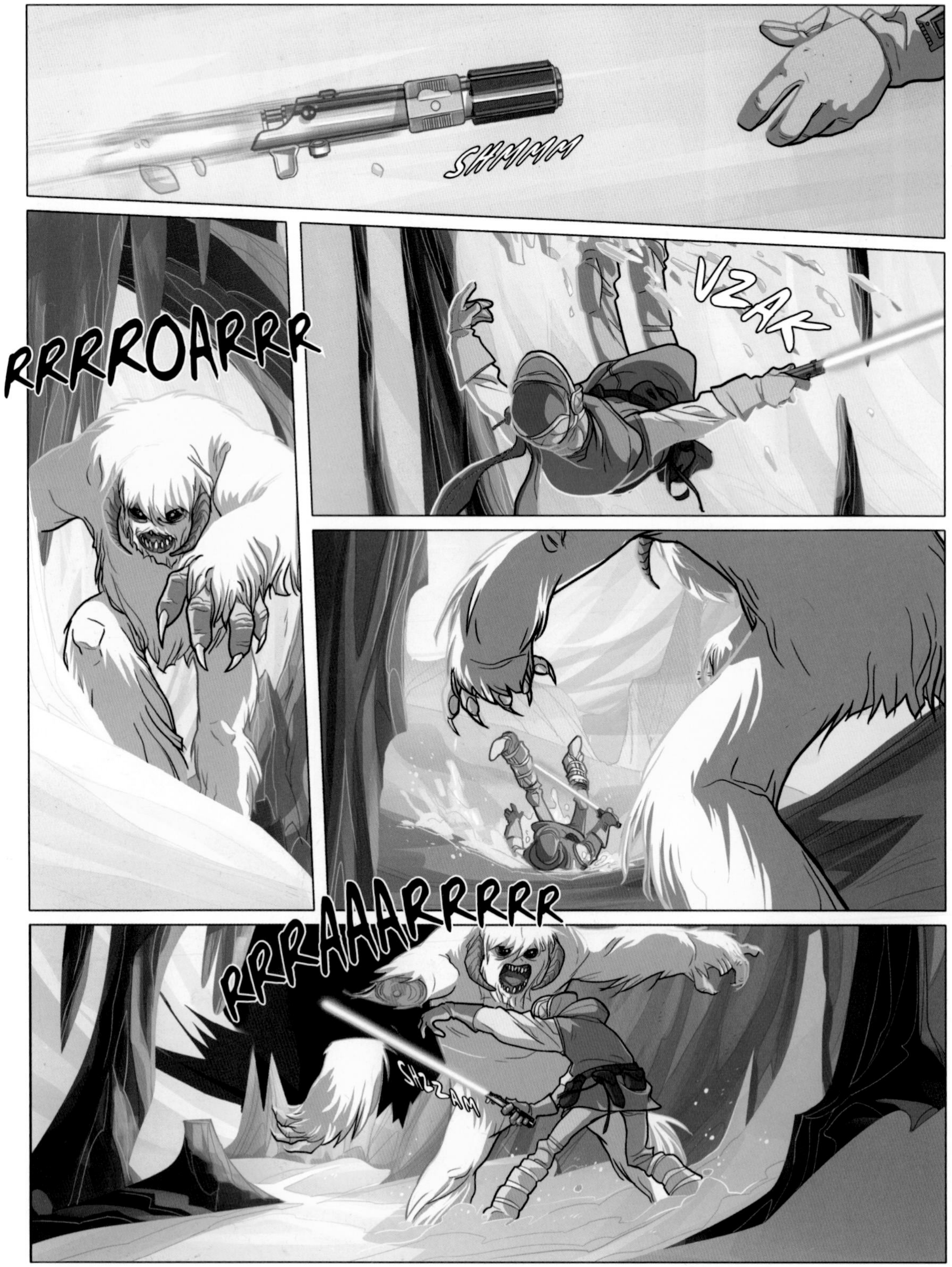
SHHMM
RRRROARRR
VZAK
RRRAAARRRRR
SHZZAM

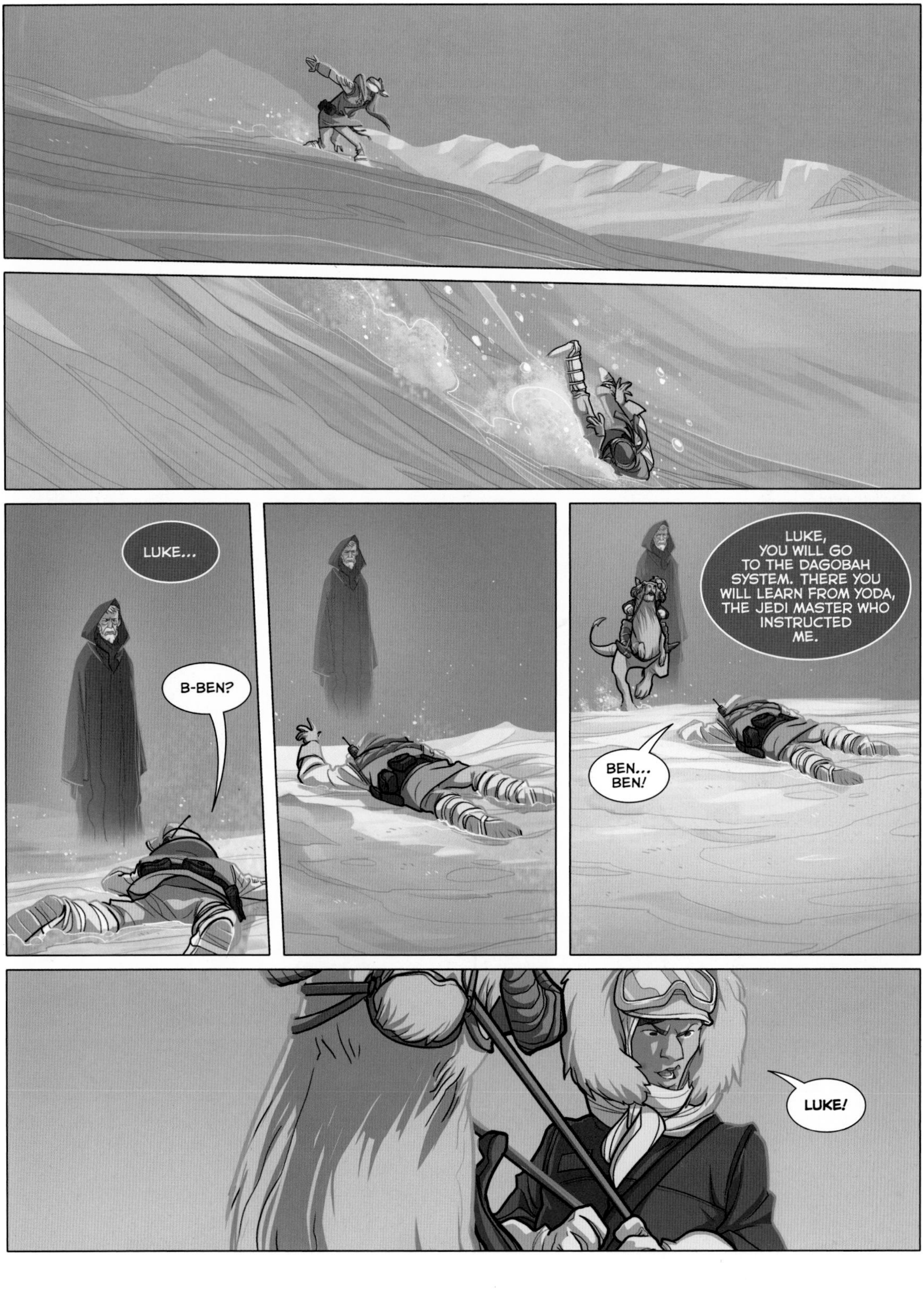
LUKE...
B-BEN?
LUKE, YOU WILL GO TO THE DAGOBAH SYSTEM. THERE YOU WILL LEARN FROM YODA, THE JEDI MASTER WHO INSTRUCTED ME.
BEN... BEN!
LUKE!

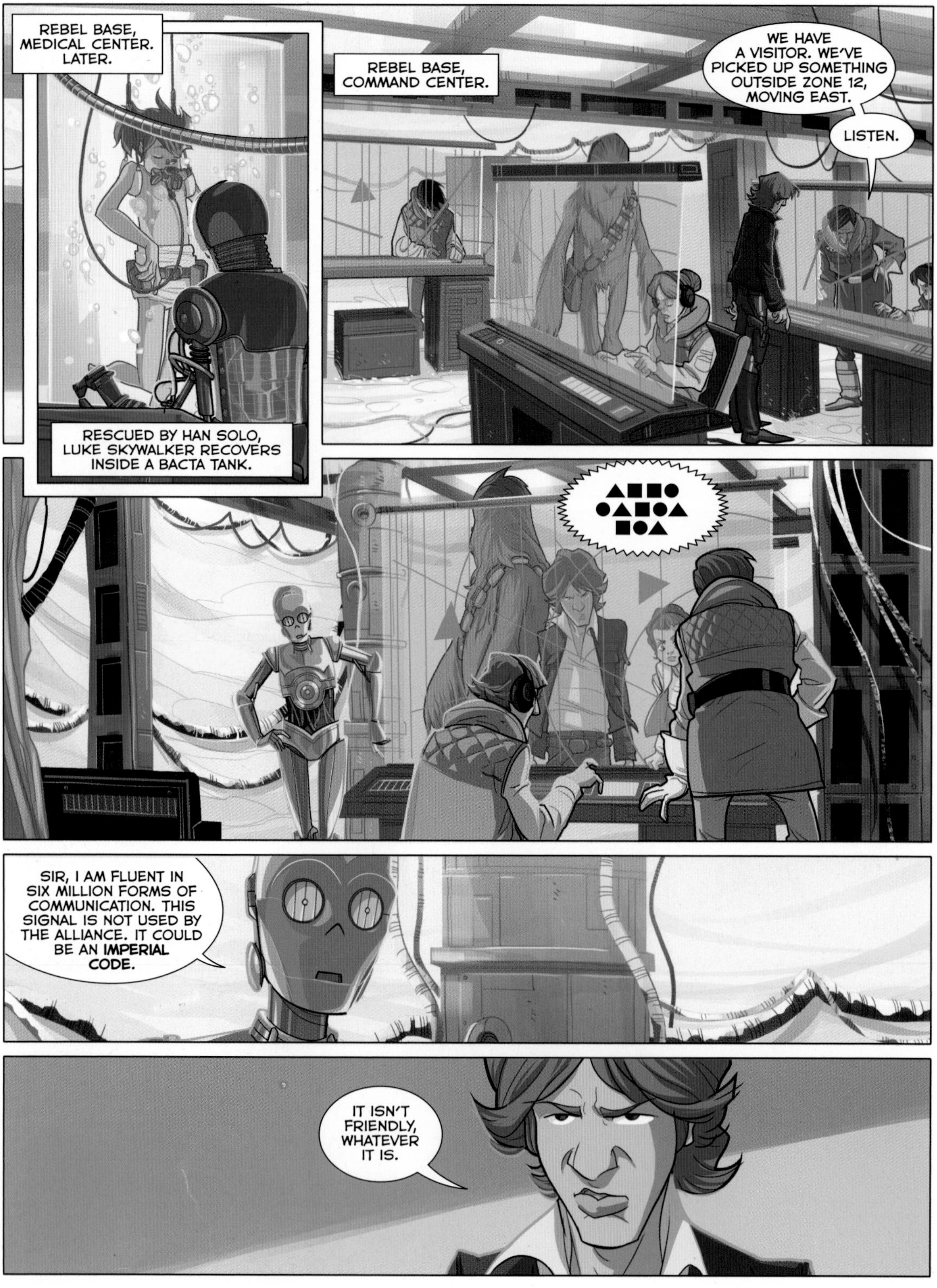
REBEL BASE, MEDICAL CENTER. LATER.
RESCUED BY HAN SOLO, LUKE SKYWALKER RECOVERS INSIDE A BACTA TANK.
REBEL BASE, COMMAND CENTER.
WE HAVE A VISITOR. WE'VE PICKED UP SOMETHING OUTSIDE ZONE 12, MOVING EAST.
LISTEN.
SIR, I AM FLUENT IN SIX MILLION FORMS OF COMMUNICATION. THIS SIGNAL IS NOT USED BY THE ALLIANCE. IT COULD BE AN **IMPERIAL CODE.**
IT ISN'T FRIENDLY, WHATEVER IT IS.

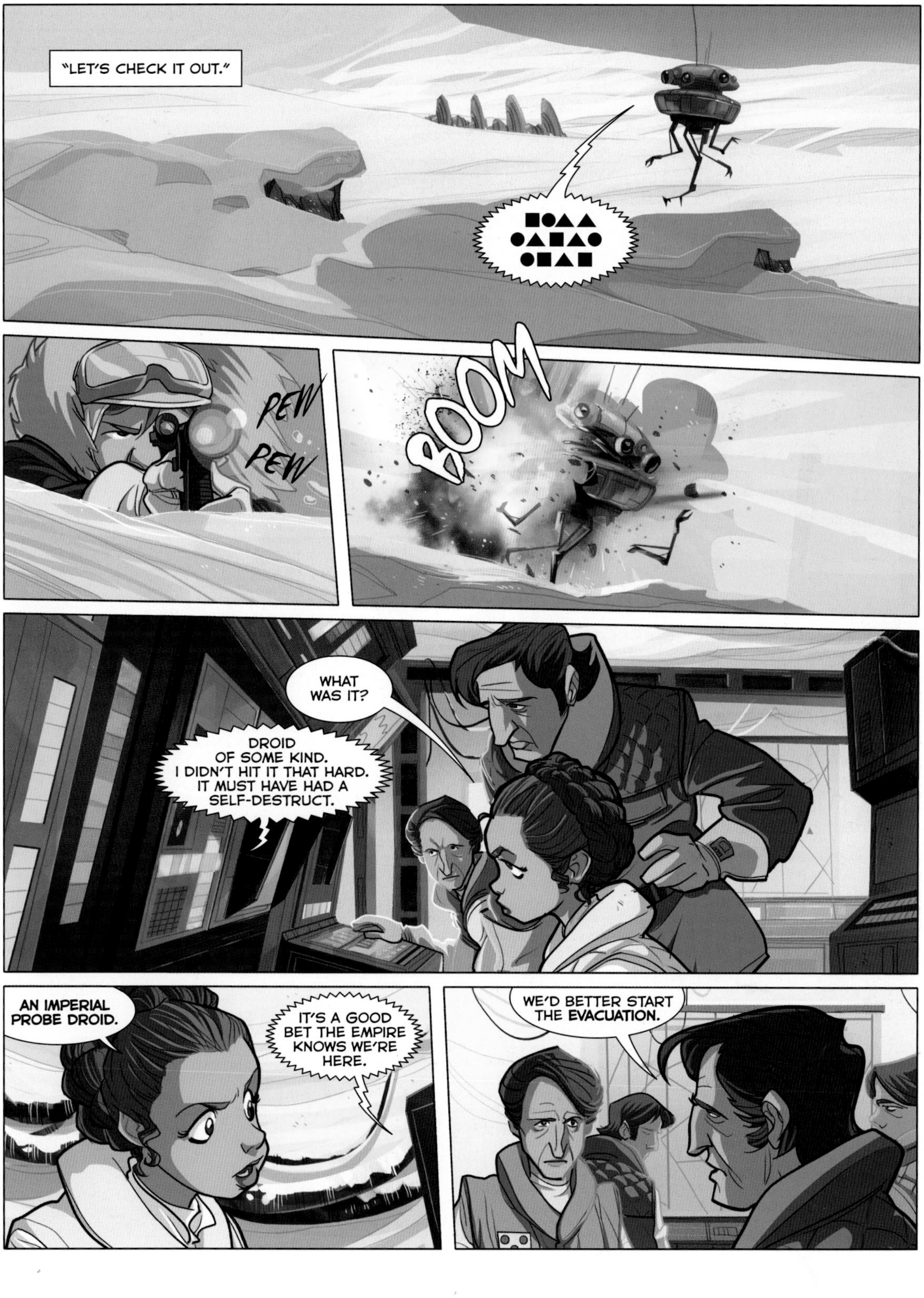
"LET'S CHECK IT OUT."
PEW
PEW
BOOM
WHAT WAS IT?
DROID OF SOME KIND. I DIDN'T HIT IT THAT HARD. IT MUST HAVE HAD A SELF-DESTRUCT.
AN IMPERIAL PROBE DROID.
IT'S A GOOD BET THE EMPIRE KNOWS WE'RE HERE.
WE'D BETTER START THE **EVACUATION**.

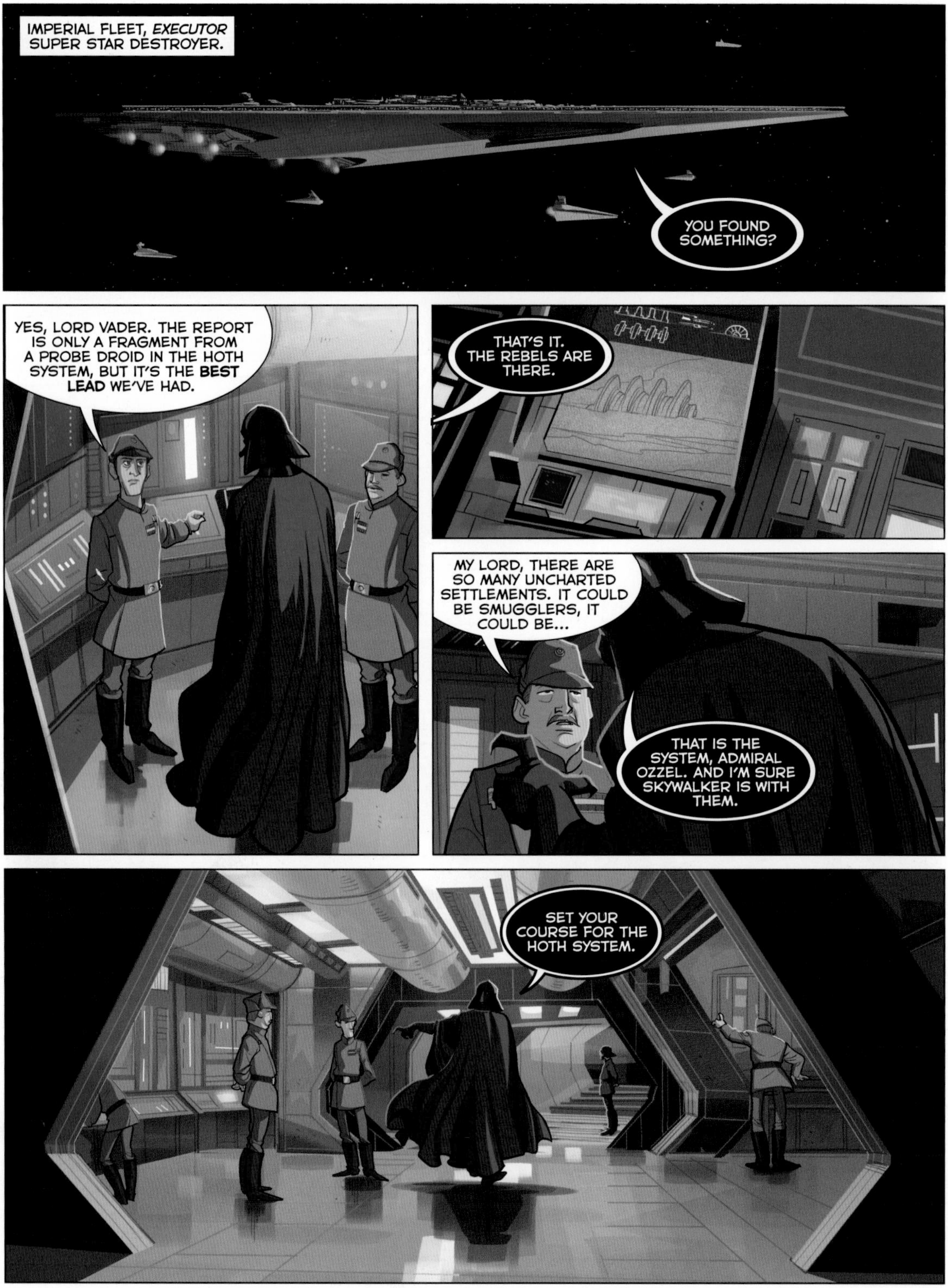
IMPERIAL FLEET, *EXECUTOR* SUPER STAR DESTROYER.
YOU FOUND SOMETHING?
YES, LORD VADER. THE REPORT IS ONLY A FRAGMENT FROM A PROBE DROID IN THE HOTH SYSTEM, BUT IT'S THE **BEST LEAD** WE'VE HAD.
THAT'S IT. THE REBELS ARE THERE.
MY LORD, THERE ARE SO MANY UNCHARTED SETTLEMENTS. IT COULD BE SMUGGLERS, IT COULD BE...
THAT IS THE SYSTEM, ADMIRAL OZZEL. AND I'M SURE SKYWALKER IS WITH THEM.
SET YOUR COURSE FOR THE HOTH SYSTEM.

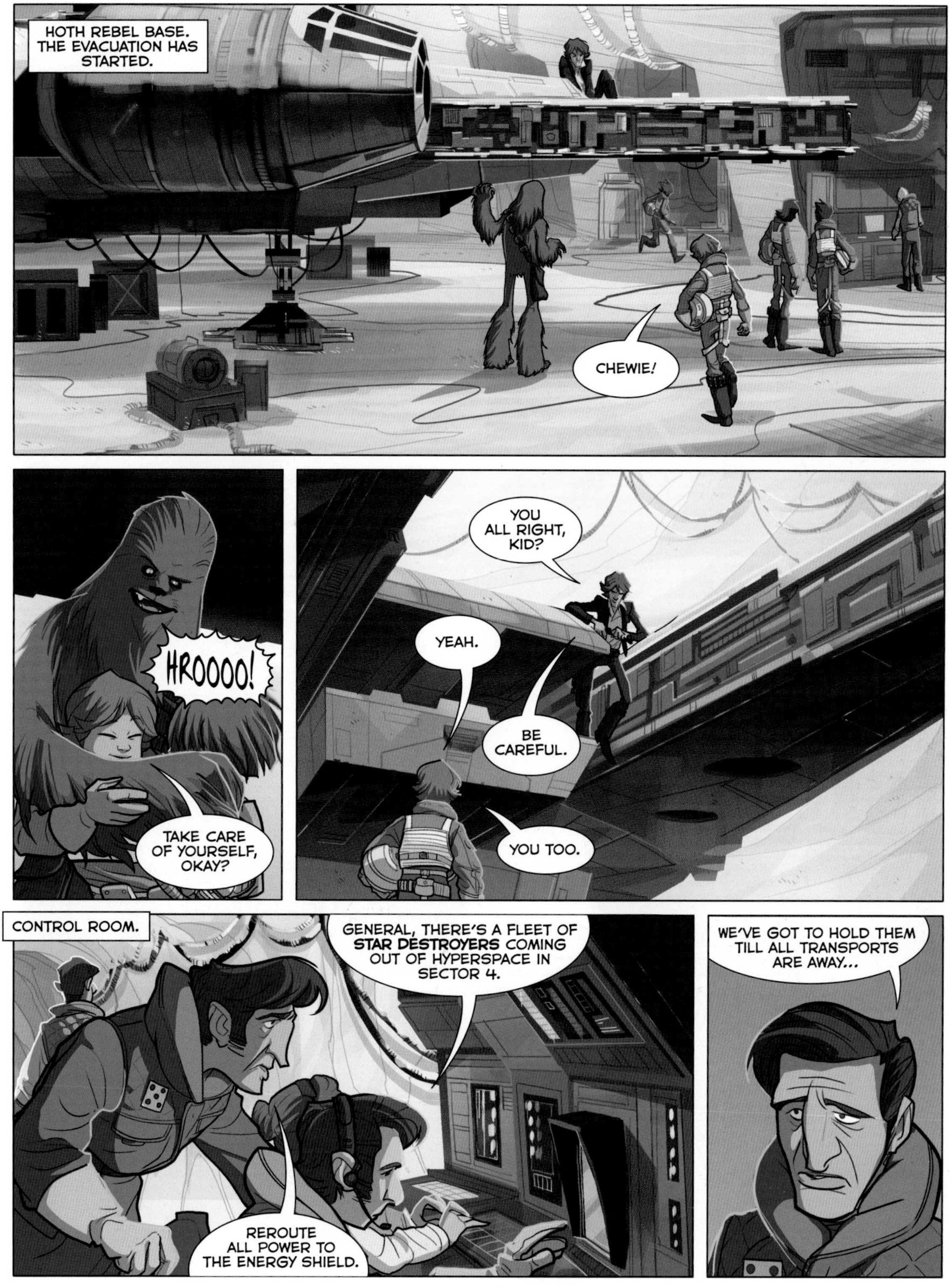
HOTH REBEL BASE. THE EVACUATION HAS STARTED.
CHEWIE!
HROOOO!
TAKE CARE OF YOURSELF, OKAY?
YOU ALL RIGHT, KID?
YEAH.
BE CAREFUL.
YOU TOO.
CONTROL ROOM.
GENERAL, THERE'S A FLEET OF **STAR DESTROYERS** COMING OUT OF HYPERSPACE IN SECTOR 4.
REROUTE ALL POWER TO THE ENERGY SHIELD.
WE'VE GOT TO HOLD THEM TILL ALL TRANSPORTS ARE AWAY...

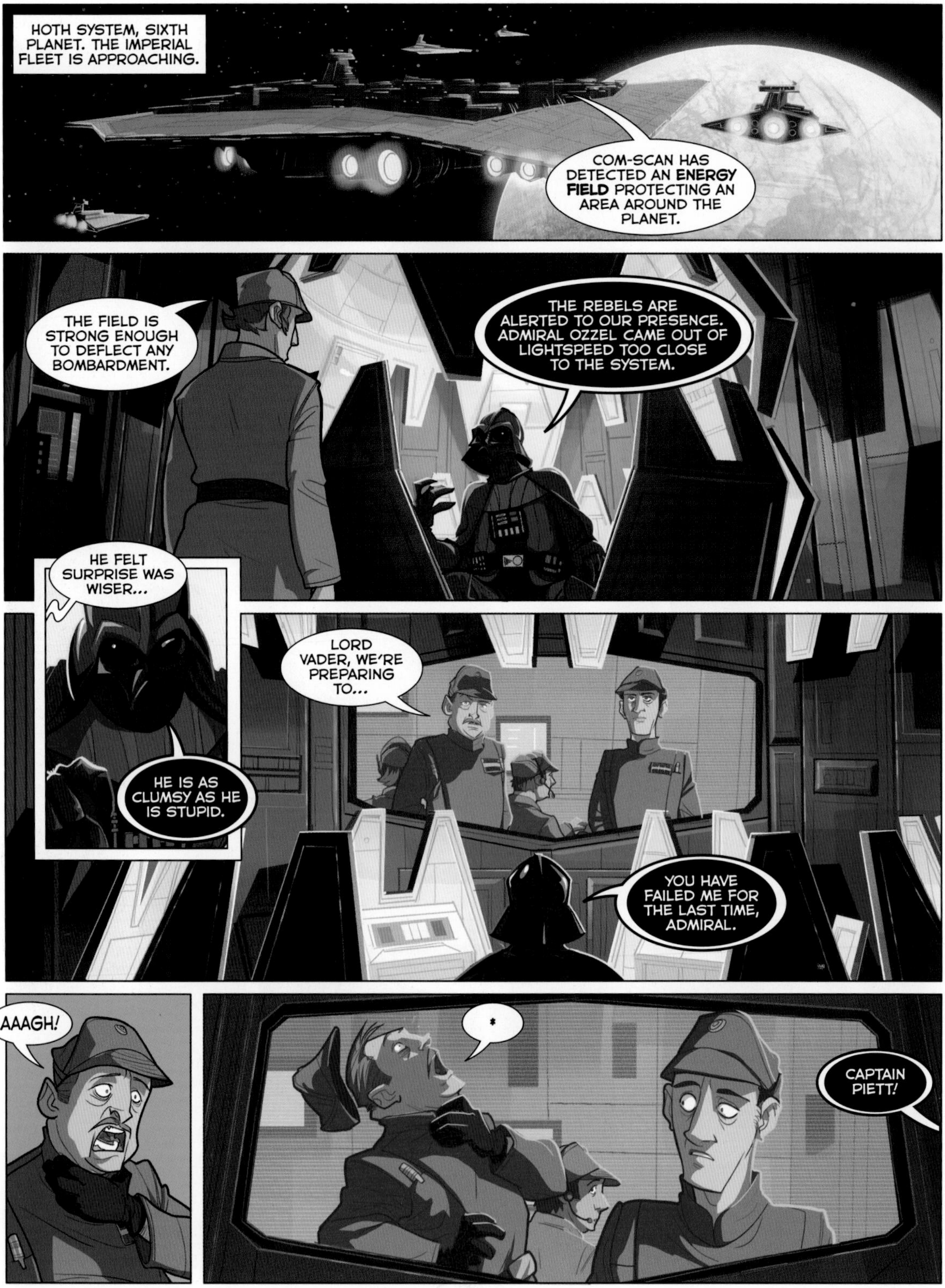
HOTH SYSTEM, SIXTH PLANET. THE IMPERIAL FLEET IS APPROACHING.
COM-SCAN HAS DETECTED AN **ENERGY FIELD** PROTECTING AN AREA AROUND THE PLANET.
THE FIELD IS STRONG ENOUGH TO DEFLECT ANY BOMBARDMENT.
THE REBELS ARE ALERTED TO OUR PRESENCE. ADMIRAL OZZEL CAME OUT OF LIGHTSPEED TOO CLOSE TO THE SYSTEM.
HE FELT SURPRISE WAS WISER...
HE IS AS CLUMSY AS HE IS STUPID.
LORD VADER, WE'RE PREPARING TO...
YOU HAVE FAILED ME FOR THE LAST TIME, ADMIRAL.
AAAGH!
*
CAPTAIN PIETT!

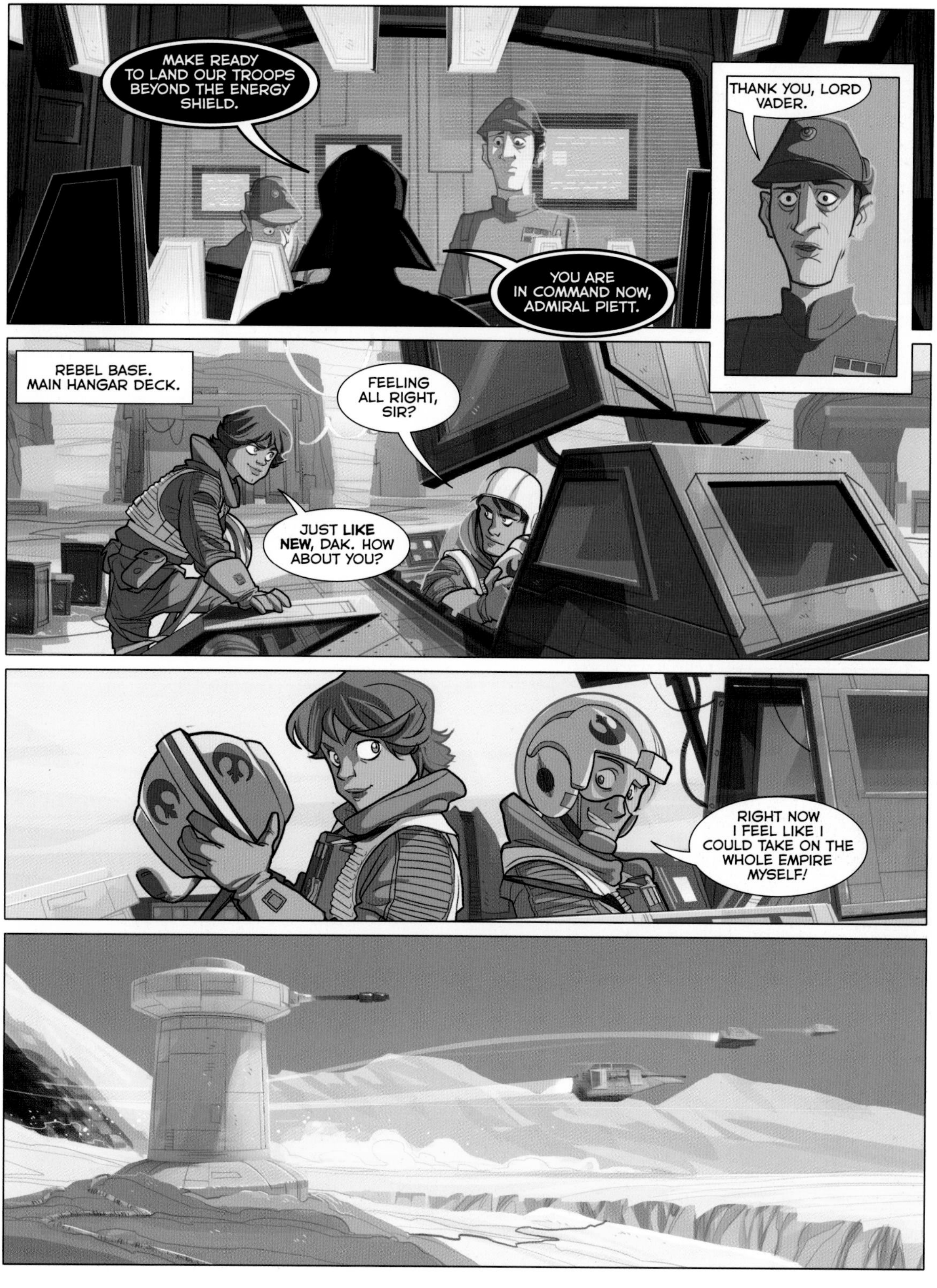
MAKE READY TO LAND OUR TROOPS BEYOND THE ENERGY SHIELD.
YOU ARE IN COMMAND NOW, ADMIRAL PIETT.
THANK YOU, LORD VADER.
REBEL BASE. MAIN HANGAR DECK.
FEELING ALL RIGHT, SIR?
JUST **LIKE NEW**, DAK. HOW ABOUT YOU?
RIGHT NOW I FEEL LIKE I COULD TAKE ON THE WHOLE EMPIRE *MYSELF!*

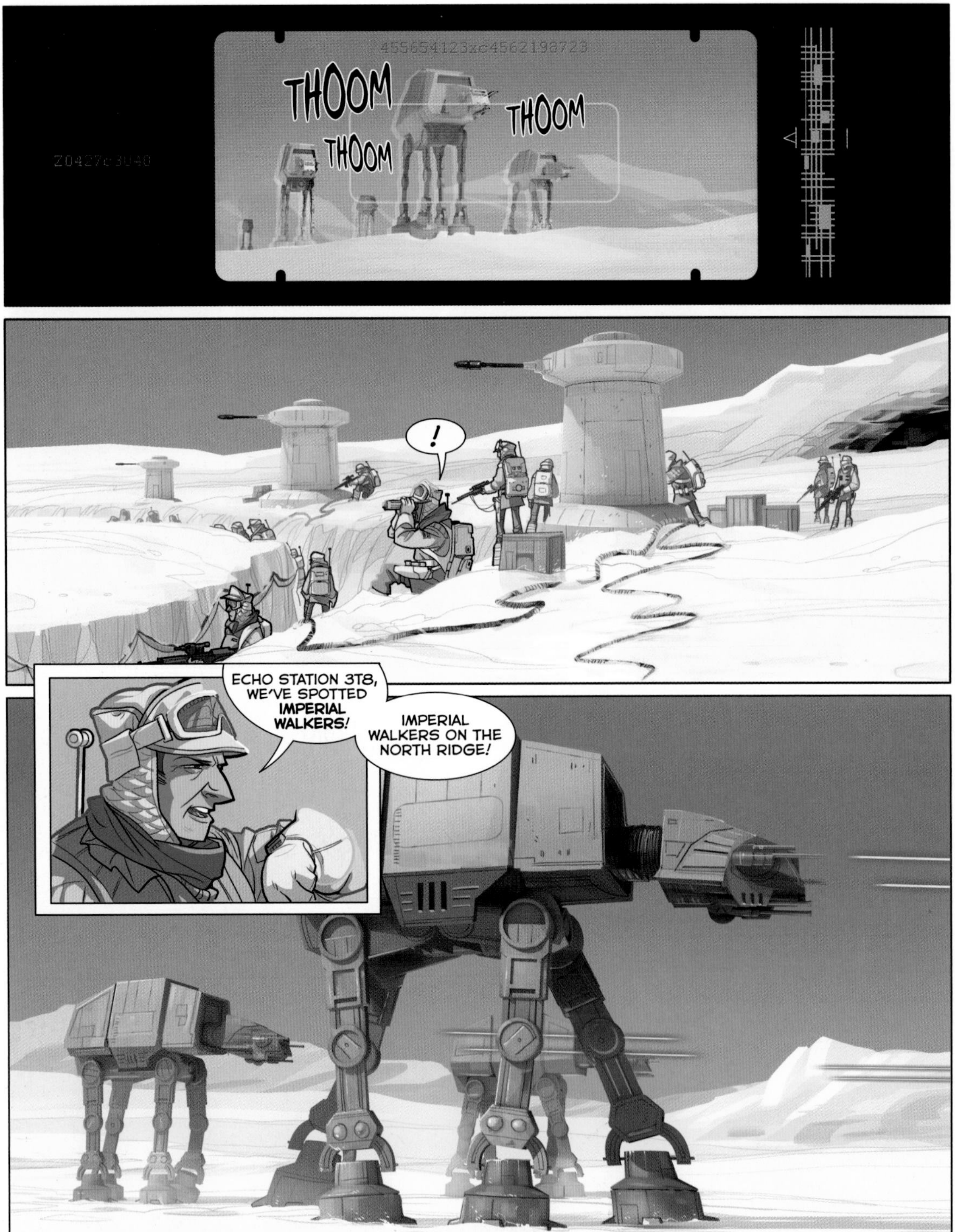
455654123xc4562198723
THOOM
THOOM
THOOM
Z0427c3040
!
ECHO STATION 3T8, WE'VE SPOTTED IMPERIAL WALKERS!
IMPERIAL WALKERS ON THE NORTH RIDGE!

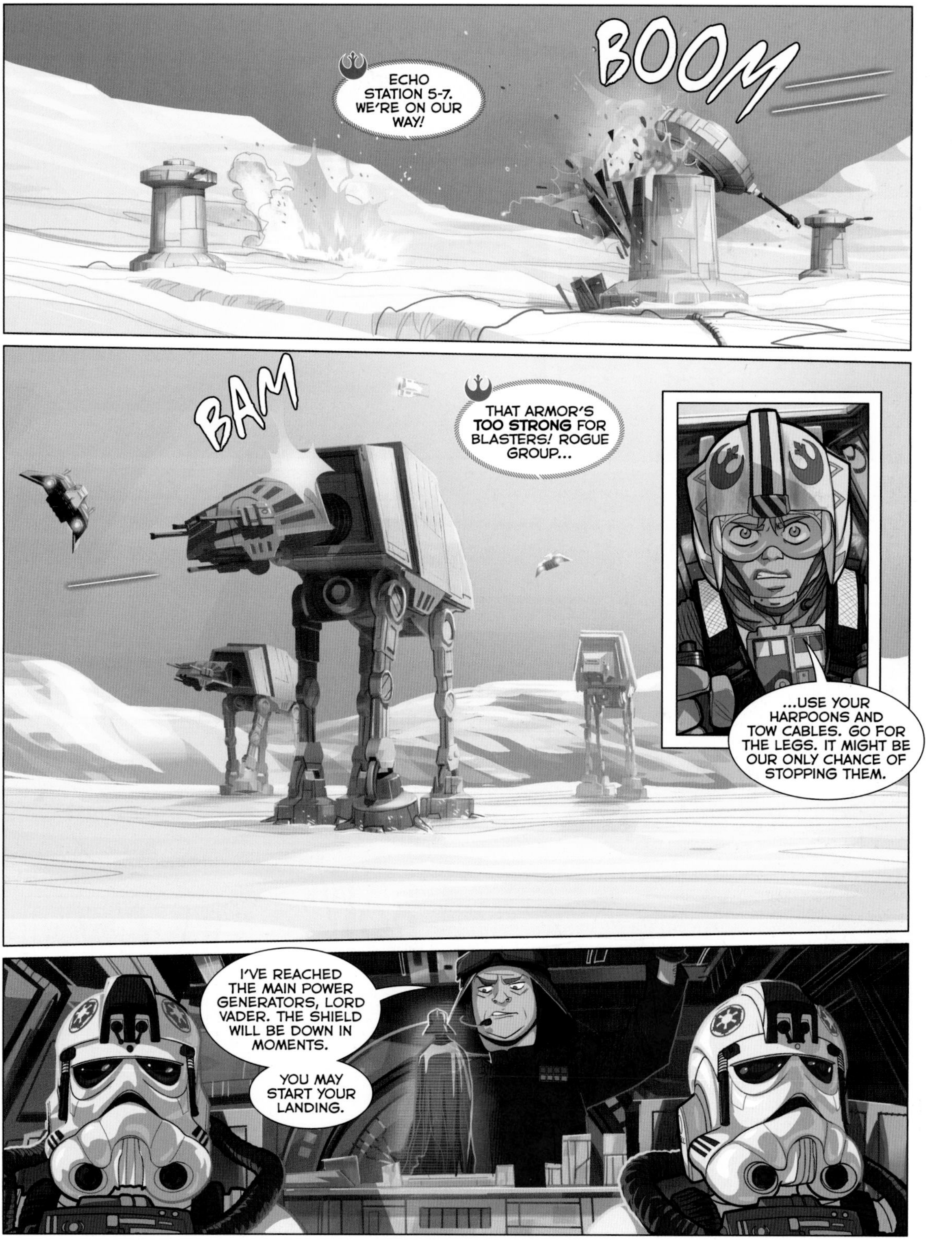

BOOM
ECHO STATION 5-7. WE'RE ON OUR WAY!
BAM
THAT ARMOR'S **TOO STRONG** FOR BLASTERS! ROGUE GROUP...
...USE YOUR HARPOONS AND TOW CABLES. GO FOR THE LEGS. IT MIGHT BE OUR ONLY CHANCE OF STOPPING THEM.
I'VE REACHED THE MAIN POWER GENERATORS, LORD VADER. THE SHIELD WILL BE DOWN IN MOMENTS.
YOU MAY START YOUR LANDING.

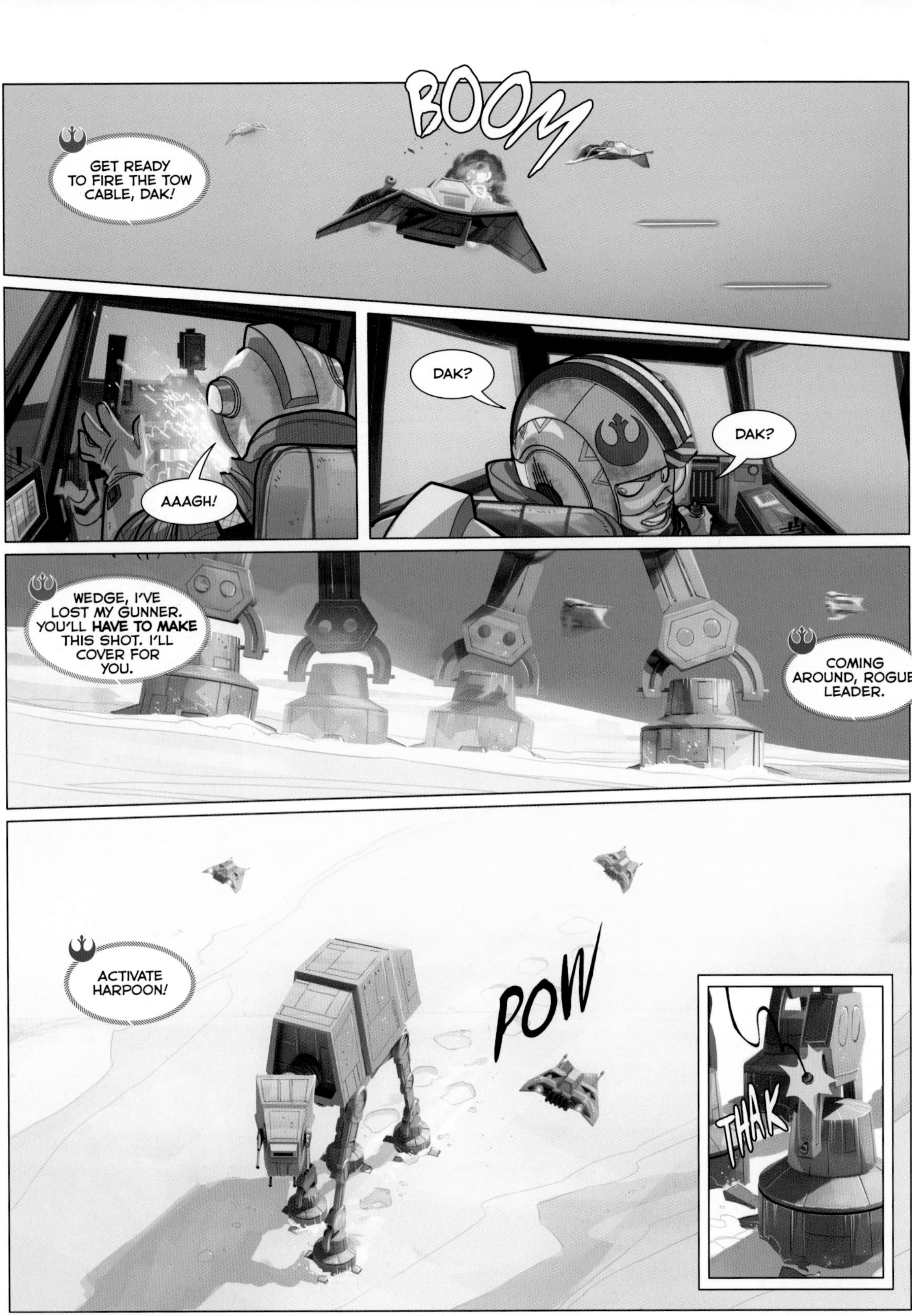
BOOM
GET READY TO FIRE THE TOW CABLE, DAK!
AAAGH!
DAK?
DAK?
WEDGE, I'VE LOST MY GUNNER. YOU'LL **HAVE TO MAKE** THIS SHOT. I'LL COVER FOR YOU.
COMING AROUND, ROGUE LEADER.
ACTIVATE HARPOON!
POW
THAK

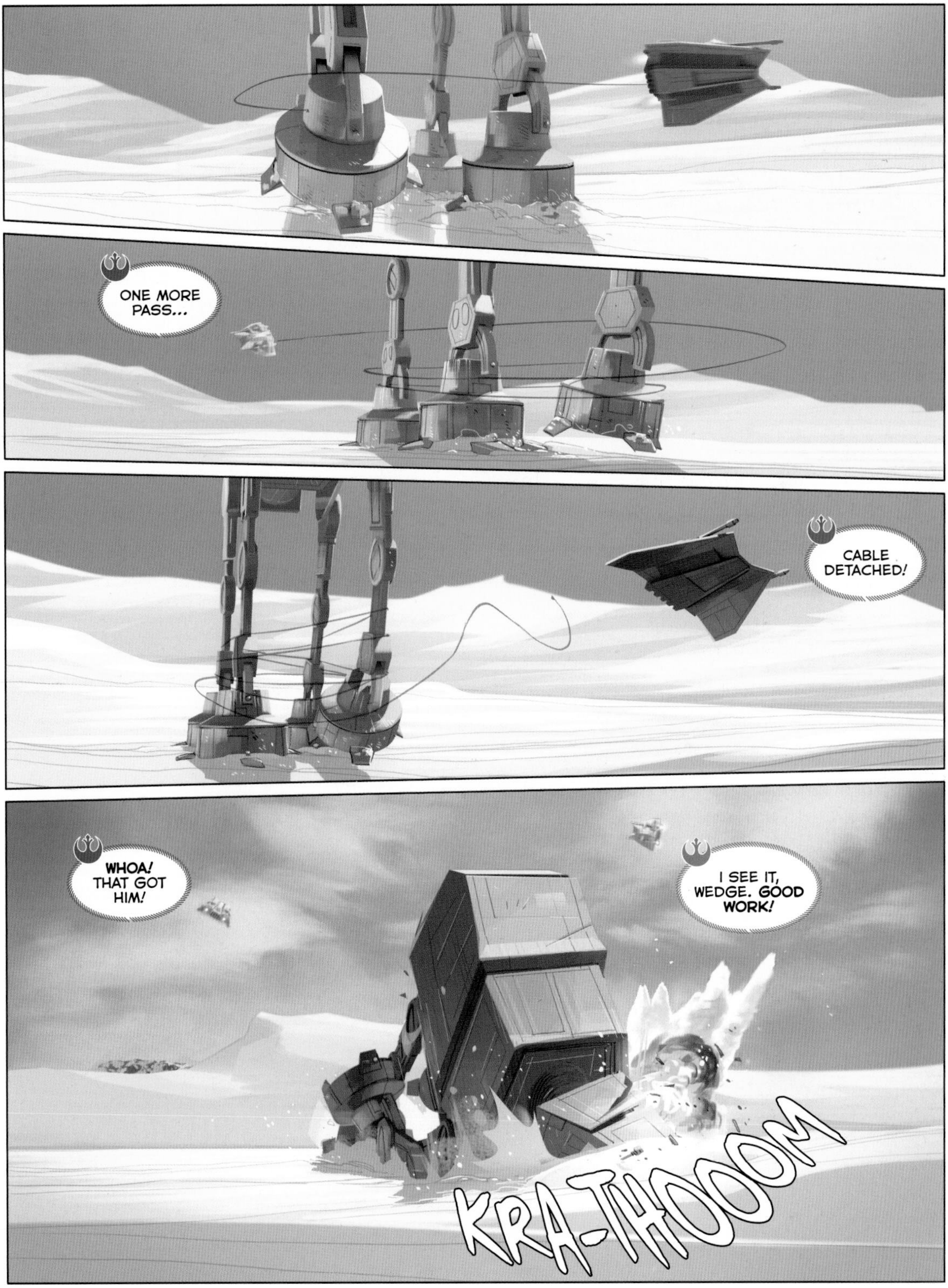
ONE MORE PASS...
CABLE DETACHED!
WHOA! THAT GOT HIM!
I SEE IT, WEDGE. GOOD WORK!
KRA-THOOOM

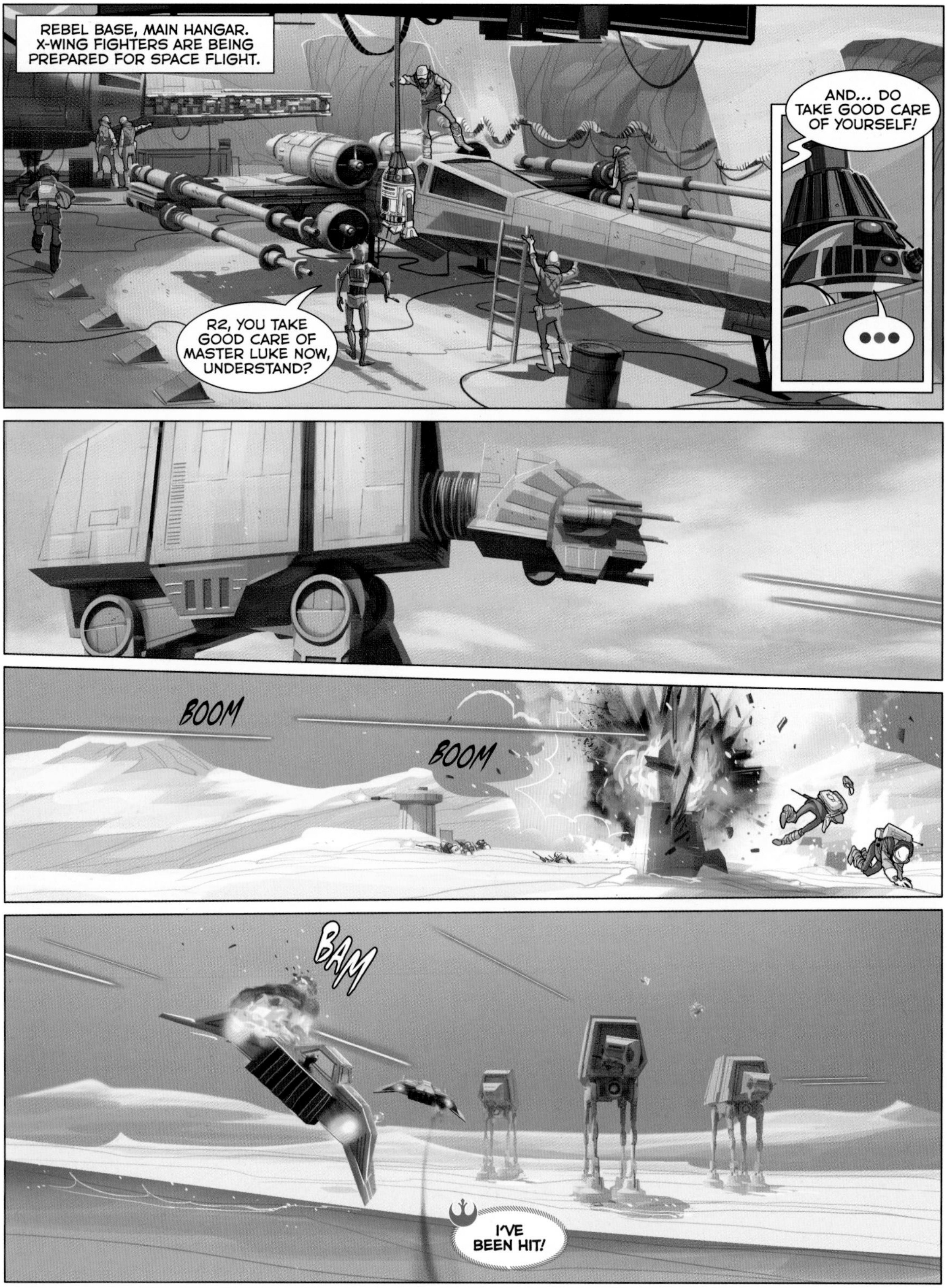
REBEL BASE, MAIN HANGAR. X-WING FIGHTERS ARE BEING PREPARED FOR SPACE FLIGHT.
R2, YOU TAKE GOOD CARE OF MASTER LUKE NOW, UNDERSTAND?
AND... DO TAKE GOOD CARE OF YOURSELF!
•••
BOOM
BOOM
BAM
I'VE BEEN HIT!

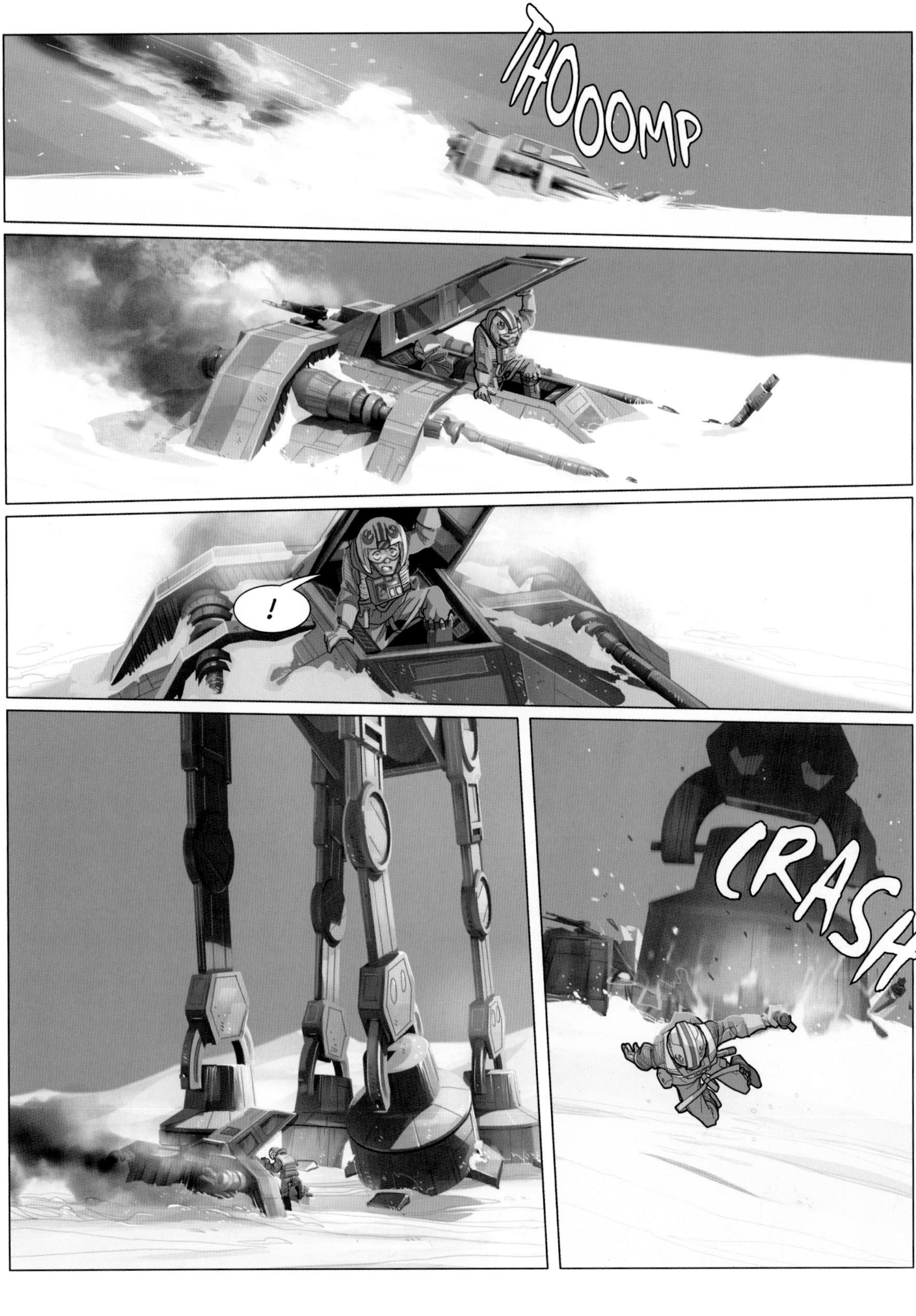
THOOOMP
!
CRASH

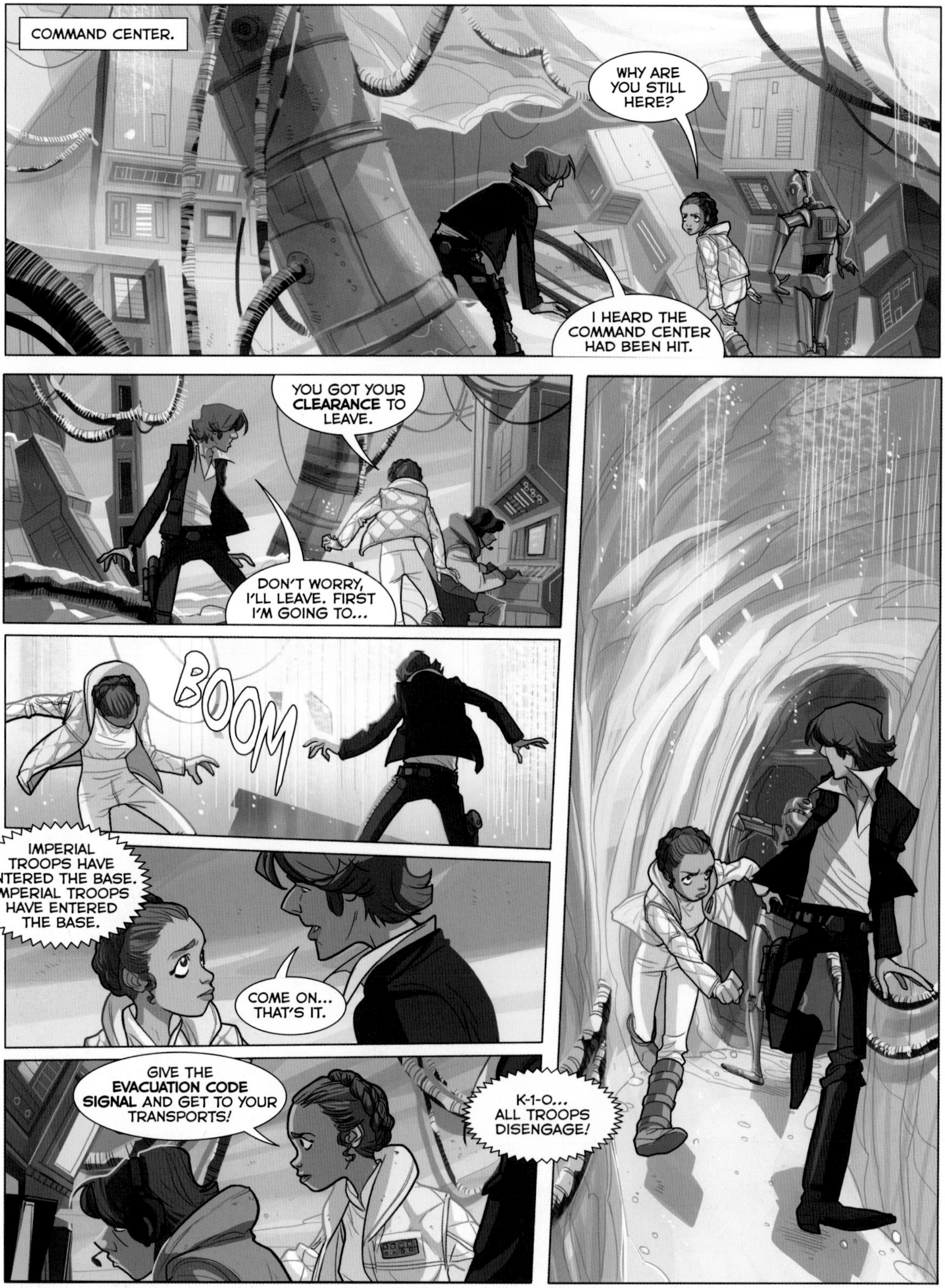
COMMAND CENTER.
WHY ARE YOU STILL HERE?
I HEARD THE COMMAND CENTER HAD BEEN HIT.
YOU GOT YOUR CLEARANCE TO LEAVE.
DON'T WORRY, I'LL LEAVE. FIRST I'M GOING TO...
BOOM
IMPERIAL TROOPS HAVE ENTERED THE BASE. IMPERIAL TROOPS HAVE ENTERED THE BASE.
COME ON... THAT'S IT.
GIVE THE EVACUATION CODE SIGNAL AND GET TO YOUR TRANSPORTS!
K-1-0... ALL TROOPS DISENGAGE!

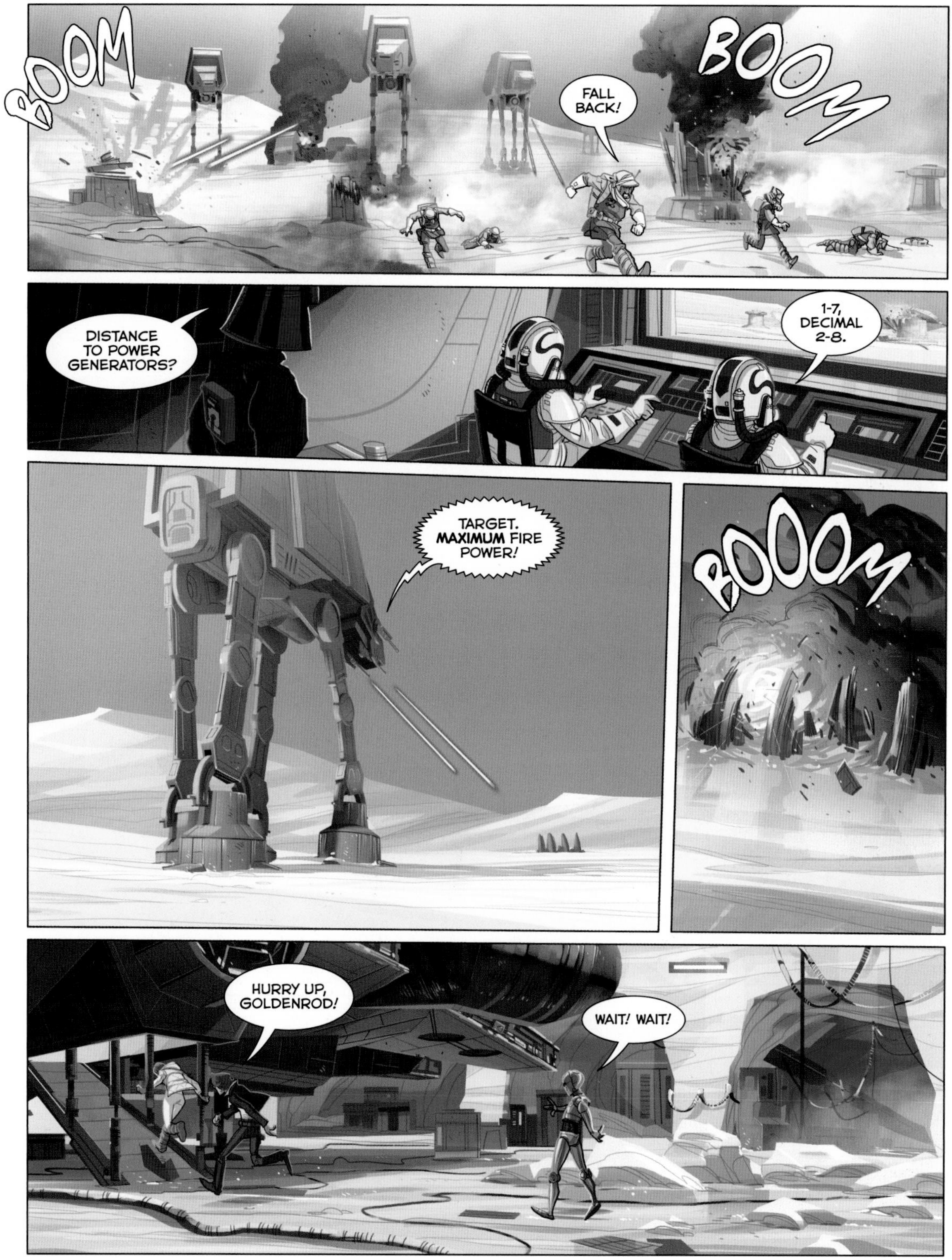
BOOM
FALL BACK!
BOOM
DISTANCE TO POWER GENERATORS?
1-7, DECIMAL 2-8.
TARGET. MAXIMUM FIRE POWER!
BOOOM
HURRY UP, GOLDENROD!
WAIT! WAIT!

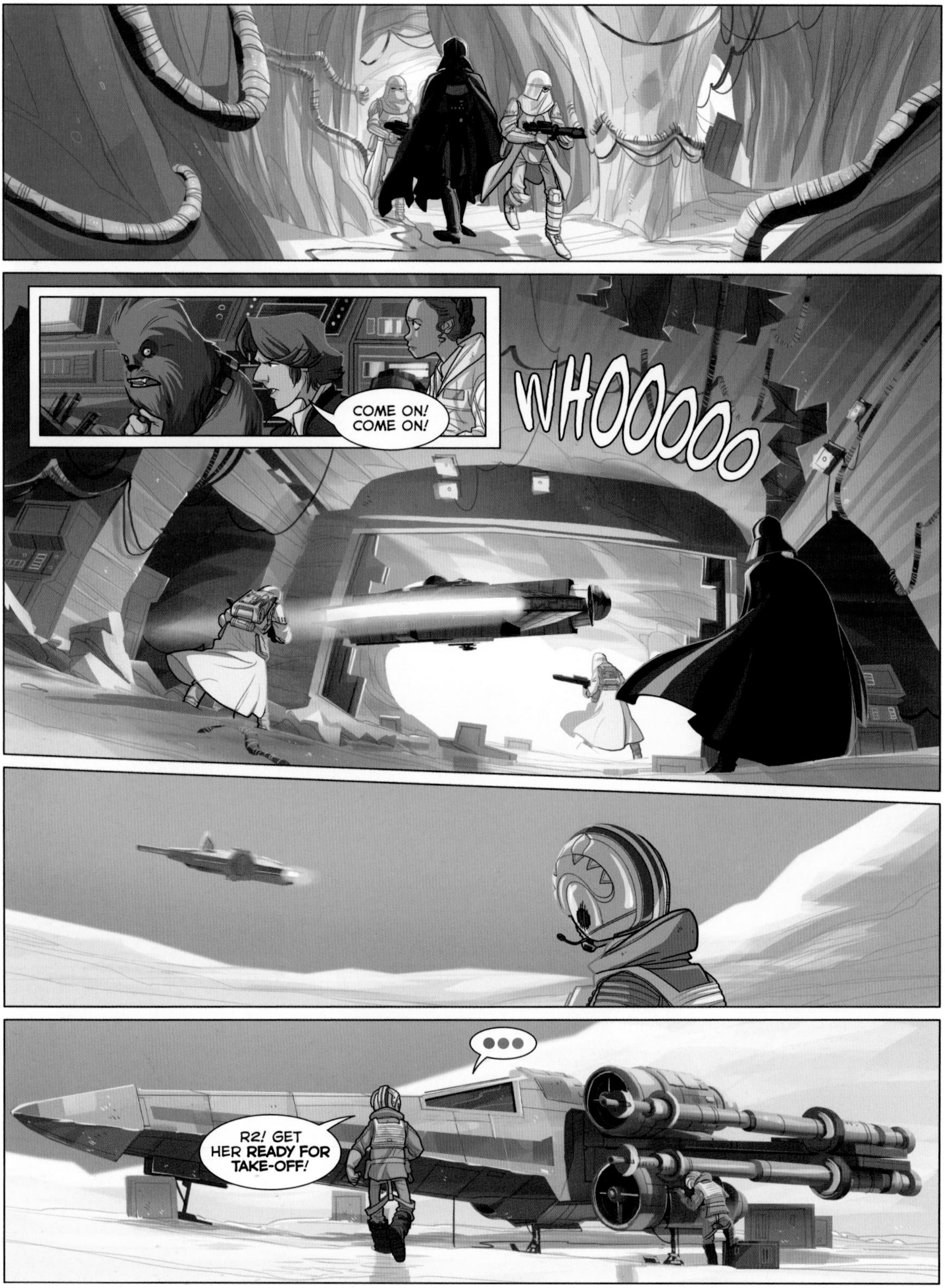
COME ON! COME ON!
WHOOOOO
•••
R2! GET HER READY FOR TAKE-OFF!

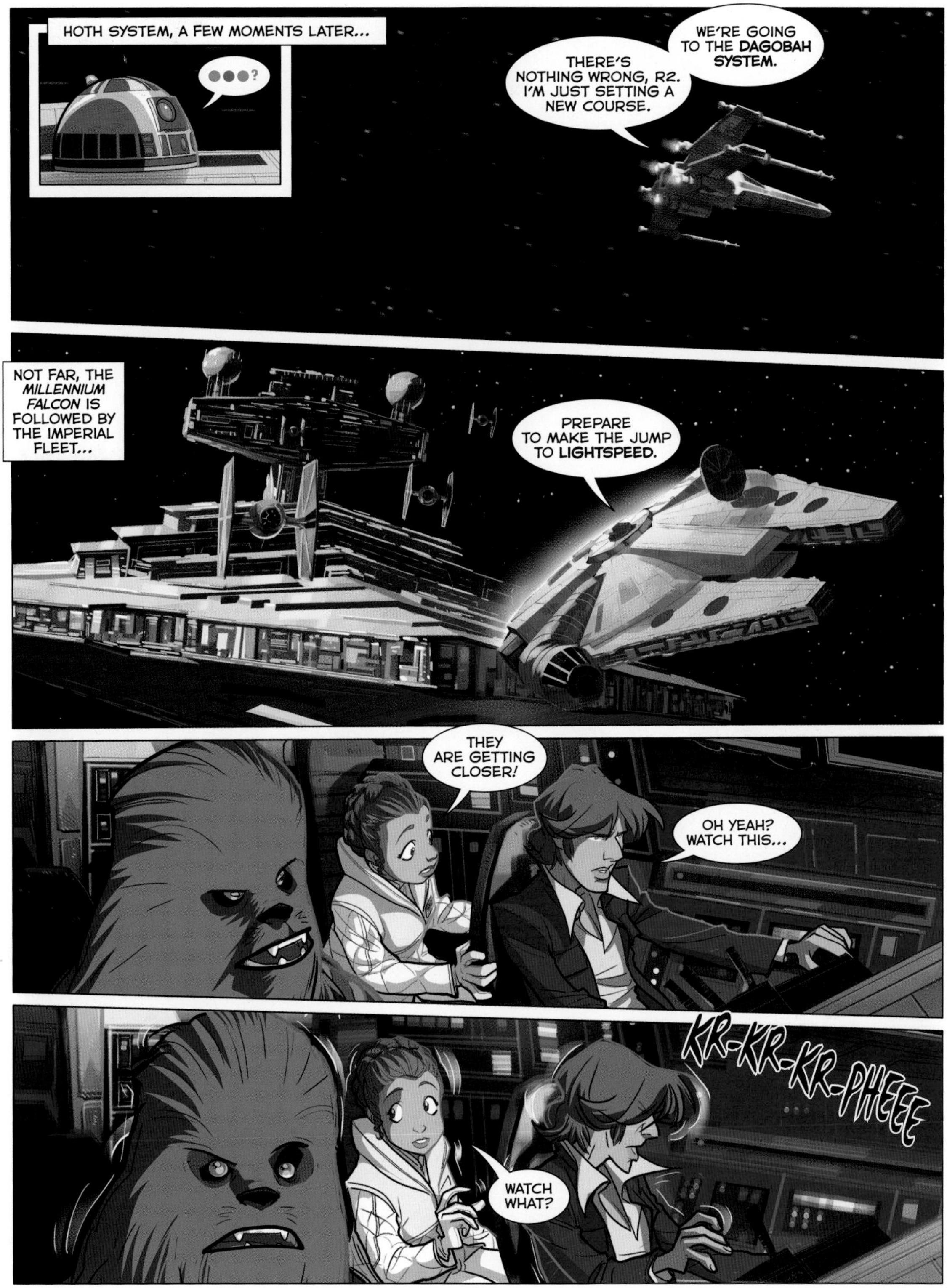

HOTH SYSTEM, A FEW MOMENTS LATER...
●●●?
THERE'S NOTHING WRONG, R2. I'M JUST SETTING A NEW COURSE.
WE'RE GOING TO THE **DAGOBAH SYSTEM.**
NOT FAR, THE *MILLENNIUM FALCON* IS FOLLOWED BY THE IMPERIAL FLEET...
PREPARE TO MAKE THE JUMP TO **LIGHTSPEED.**
THEY ARE GETTING CLOSER!
OH YEAH? WATCH THIS...
KR-KR-KR-PHEEE
WATCH WHAT?

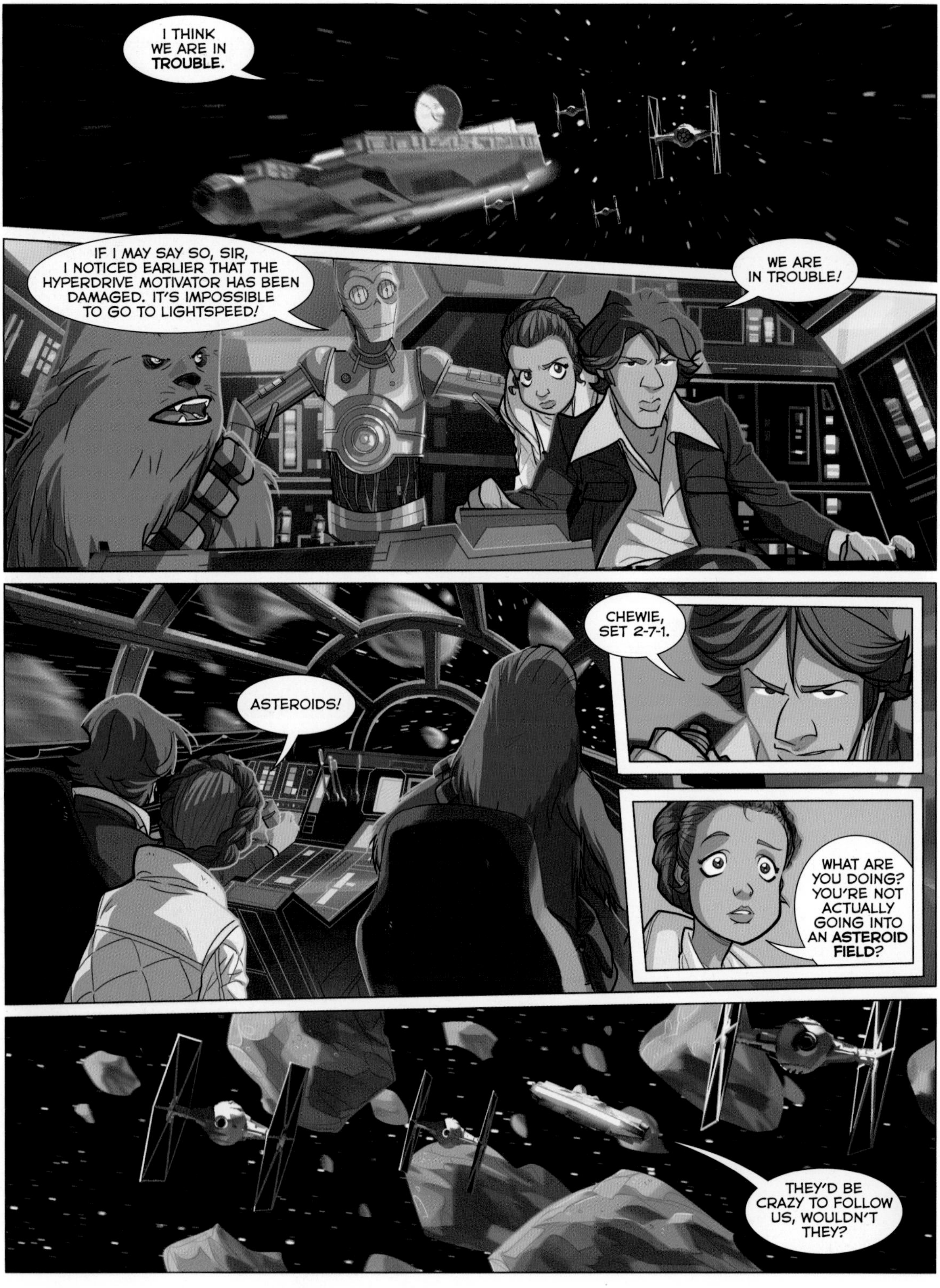
I THINK WE ARE IN TROUBLE.
IF I MAY SAY SO, SIR, I NOTICED EARLIER THAT THE HYPERDRIVE MOTIVATOR HAS BEEN DAMAGED. IT'S IMPOSSIBLE TO GO TO LIGHTSPEED!
WE ARE IN TROUBLE!
ASTEROIDS!
CHEWIE, SET 2-7-1.
WHAT ARE YOU DOING? YOU'RE NOT ACTUALLY GOING INTO AN ASTEROID FIELD?
THEY'D BE CRAZY TO FOLLOW US, WOULDN'T THEY?

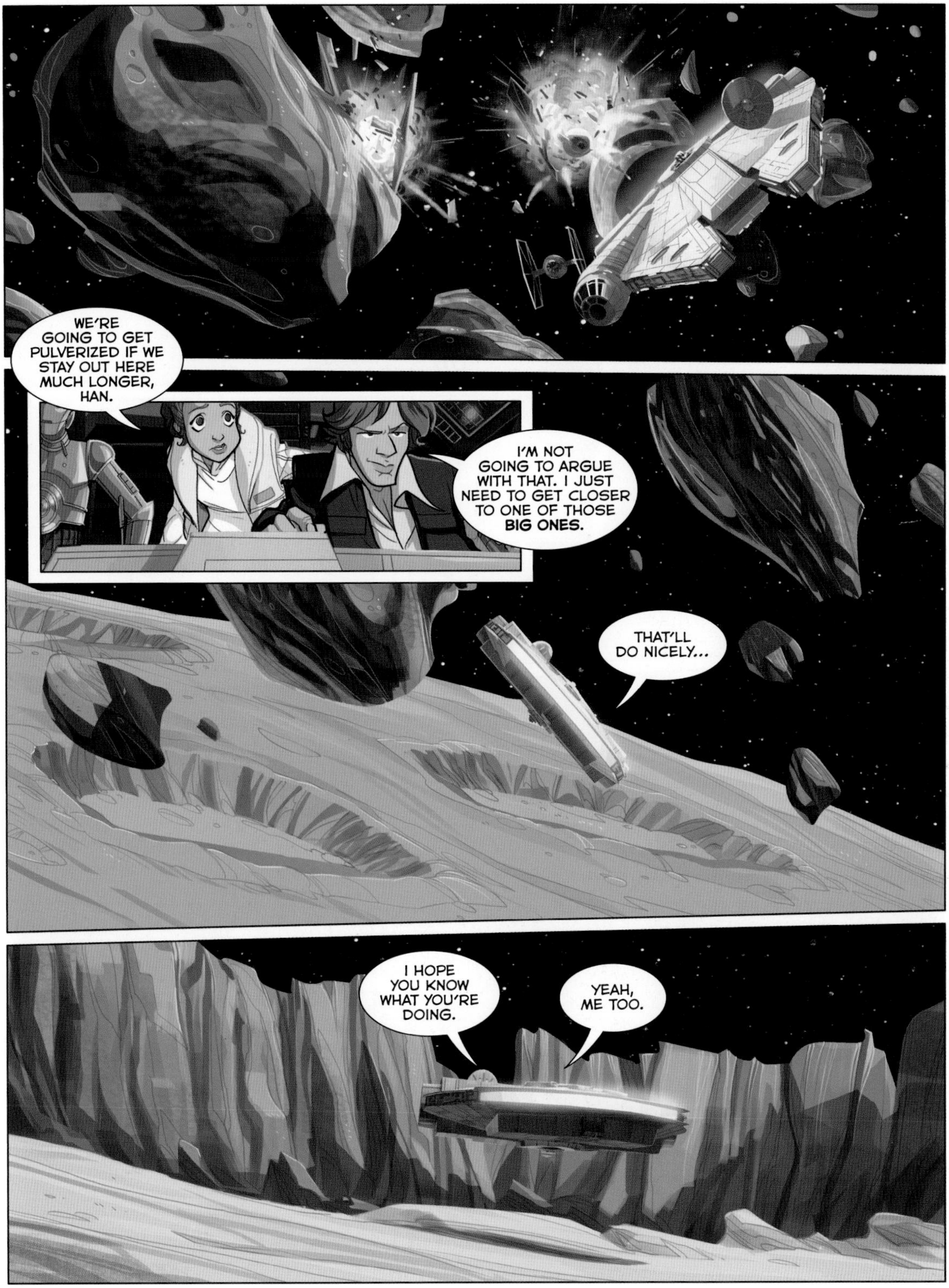
WE'RE GOING TO GET PULVERIZED IF WE STAY OUT HERE MUCH LONGER, HAN.
I'M NOT GOING TO ARGUE WITH THAT. I JUST NEED TO GET CLOSER TO ONE OF THOSE **BIG ONES.**
THAT'LL DO NICELY...
I HOPE YOU KNOW WHAT YOU'RE DOING.
YEAH, ME TOO.

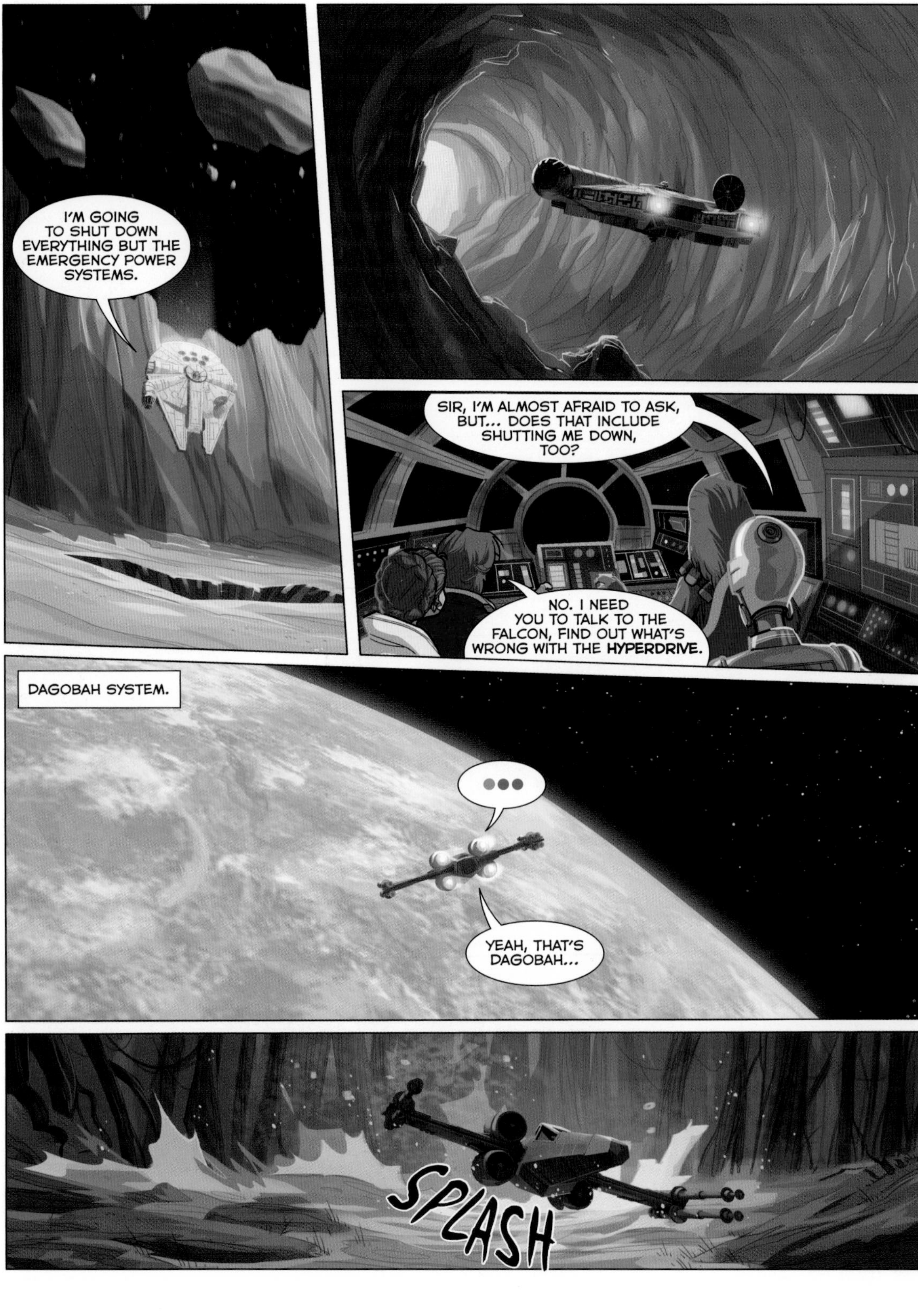
I'M GOING TO SHUT DOWN EVERYTHING BUT THE EMERGENCY POWER SYSTEMS.
SIR, I'M ALMOST AFRAID TO ASK, BUT... DOES THAT INCLUDE SHUTTING ME DOWN, TOO?
NO. I NEED YOU TO TALK TO THE FALCON, FIND OUT WHAT'S WRONG WITH THE **HYPERDRIVE**.
DAGOBAH SYSTEM.
•••
YEAH, THAT'S DAGOBAH...
SPLASH

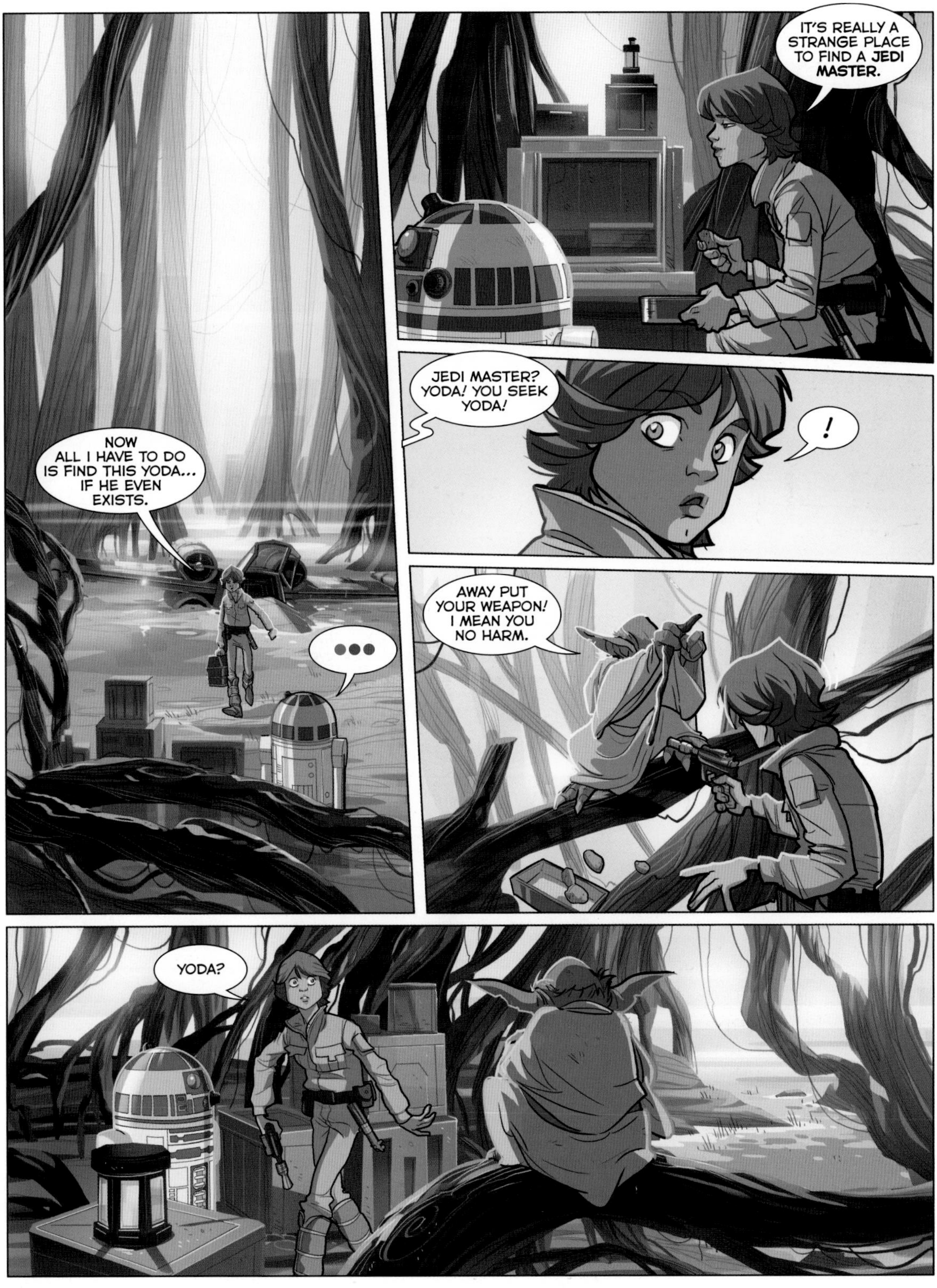
NOW ALL I HAVE TO DO IS FIND THIS YODA... IF HE EVEN EXISTS.
•••
IT'S REALLY A STRANGE PLACE TO FIND A JEDI MASTER.
JEDI MASTER? YODA! YOU SEEK YODA!
!
AWAY PUT YOUR WEAPON! I MEAN YOU NO HARM.
YODA?

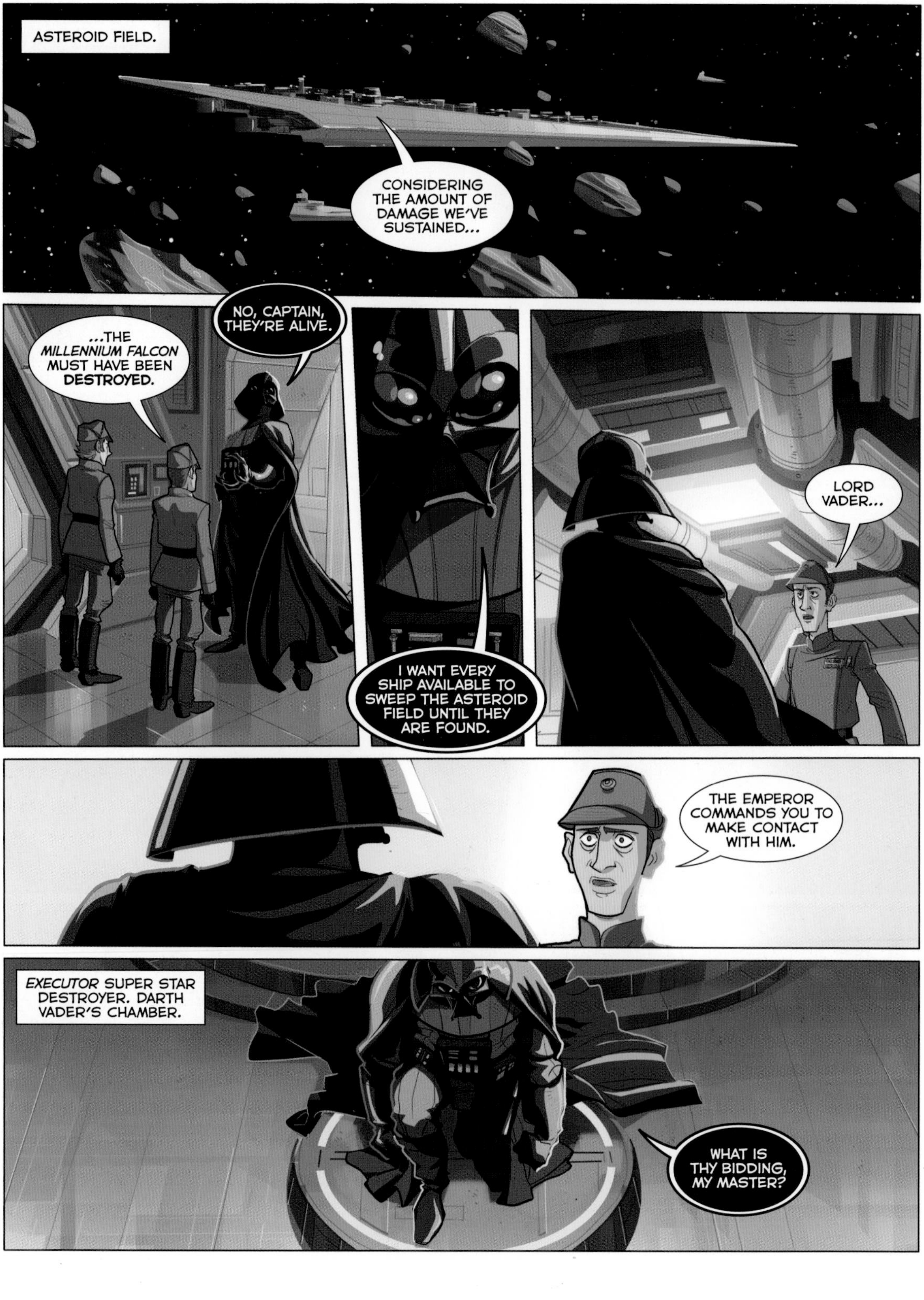
ASTEROID FIELD.
CONSIDERING THE AMOUNT OF DAMAGE WE'VE SUSTAINED...
...THE MILLENNIUM FALCON MUST HAVE BEEN DESTROYED.
NO, CAPTAIN, THEY'RE ALIVE.
I WANT EVERY SHIP AVAILABLE TO SWEEP THE ASTEROID FIELD UNTIL THEY ARE FOUND.
LORD VADER...
THE EMPEROR COMMANDS YOU TO MAKE CONTACT WITH HIM.
EXECUTOR SUPER STAR DESTROYER. DARTH VADER'S CHAMBER.
WHAT IS THY BIDDING, MY MASTER?

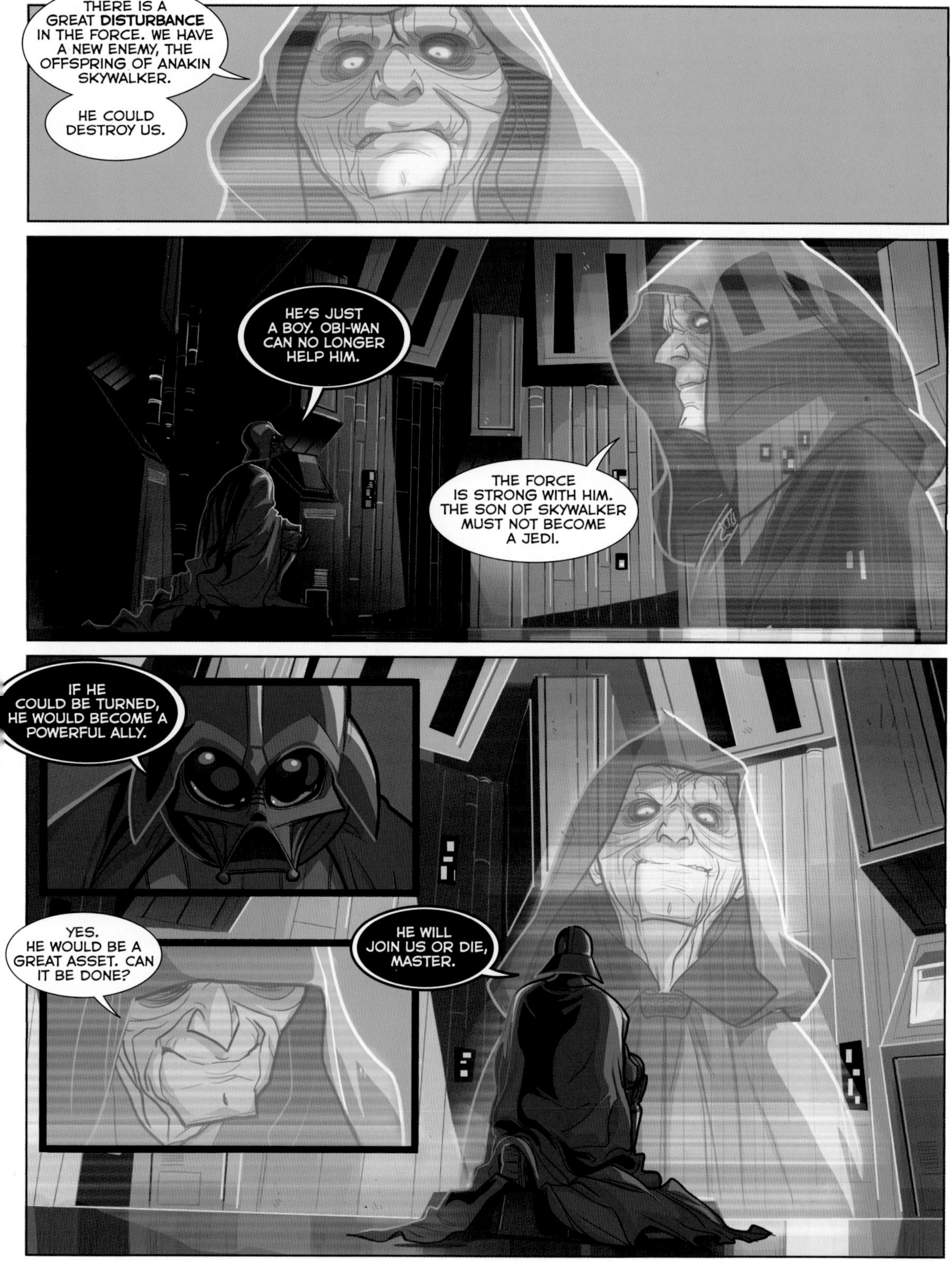
THERE IS A GREAT DISTURBANCE IN THE FORCE. WE HAVE A NEW ENEMY, THE OFFSPRING OF ANAKIN SKYWALKER.
HE COULD DESTROY US.
HE'S JUST A BOY. OBI-WAN CAN NO LONGER HELP HIM.
THE FORCE IS STRONG WITH HIM. THE SON OF SKYWALKER MUST NOT BECOME A JEDI.
IF HE COULD BE TURNED, HE WOULD BECOME A POWERFUL ALLY.
YES. HE WOULD BE A GREAT ASSET. CAN IT BE DONE?
HE WILL JOIN US OR DIE, MASTER.

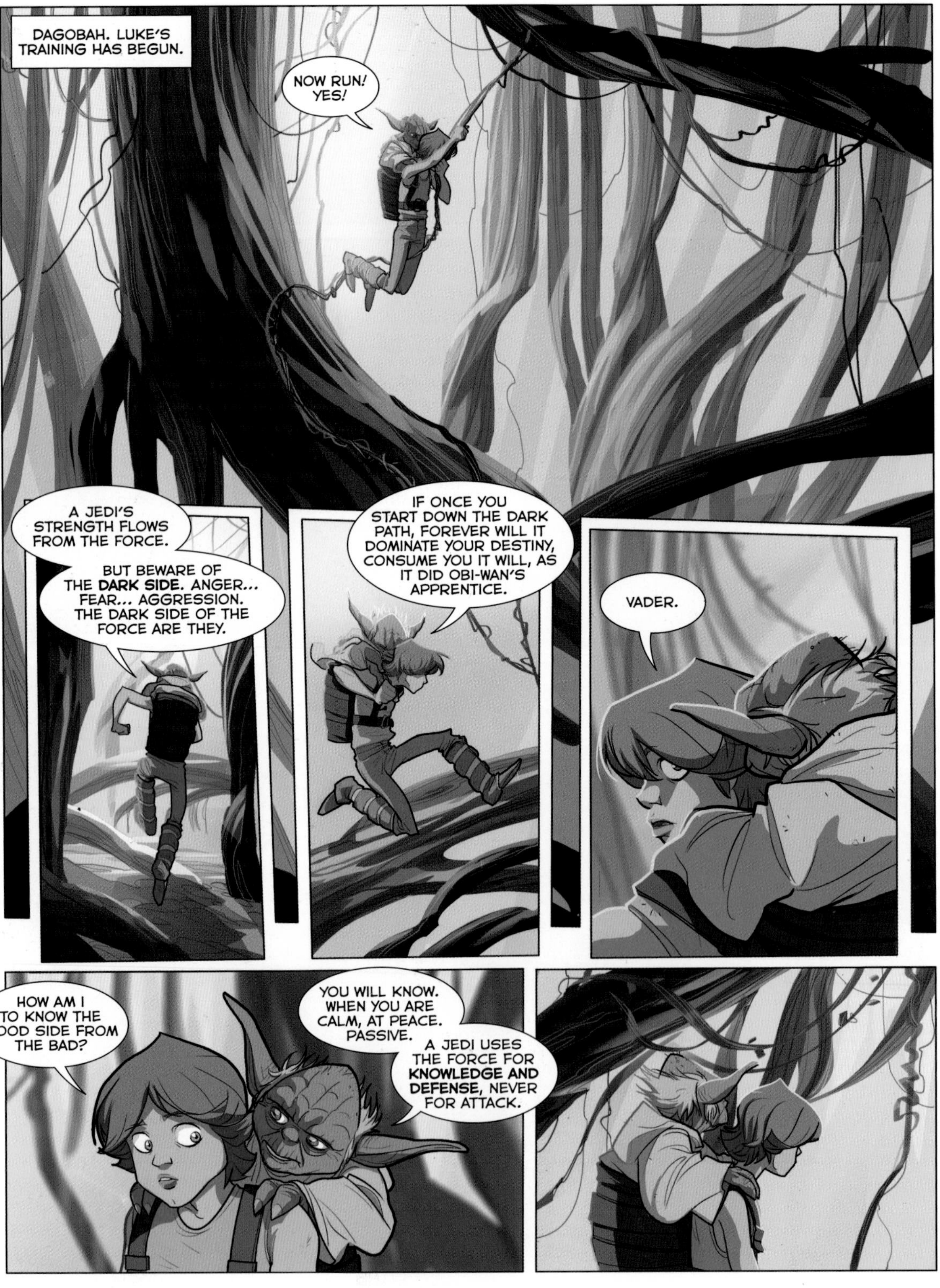

DAGOBAH. LUKE'S TRAINING HAS BEGUN.
NOW RUN! YES!
A JEDI'S STRENGTH FLOWS FROM THE FORCE.
BUT BEWARE OF THE **DARK SIDE.** ANGER... FEAR... AGGRESSION. THE DARK SIDE OF THE FORCE ARE THEY.
IF ONCE YOU START DOWN THE DARK PATH, FOREVER WILL IT DOMINATE YOUR DESTINY, CONSUME YOU IT WILL, AS IT DID OBI-WAN'S APPRENTICE.
VADER.
HOW AM I TO KNOW THE GOOD SIDE FROM THE BAD?
YOU WILL KNOW. WHEN YOU ARE CALM, AT PEACE. PASSIVE.
A JEDI USES THE FORCE FOR **KNOWLEDGE AND DEFENSE,** NEVER FOR ATTACK.

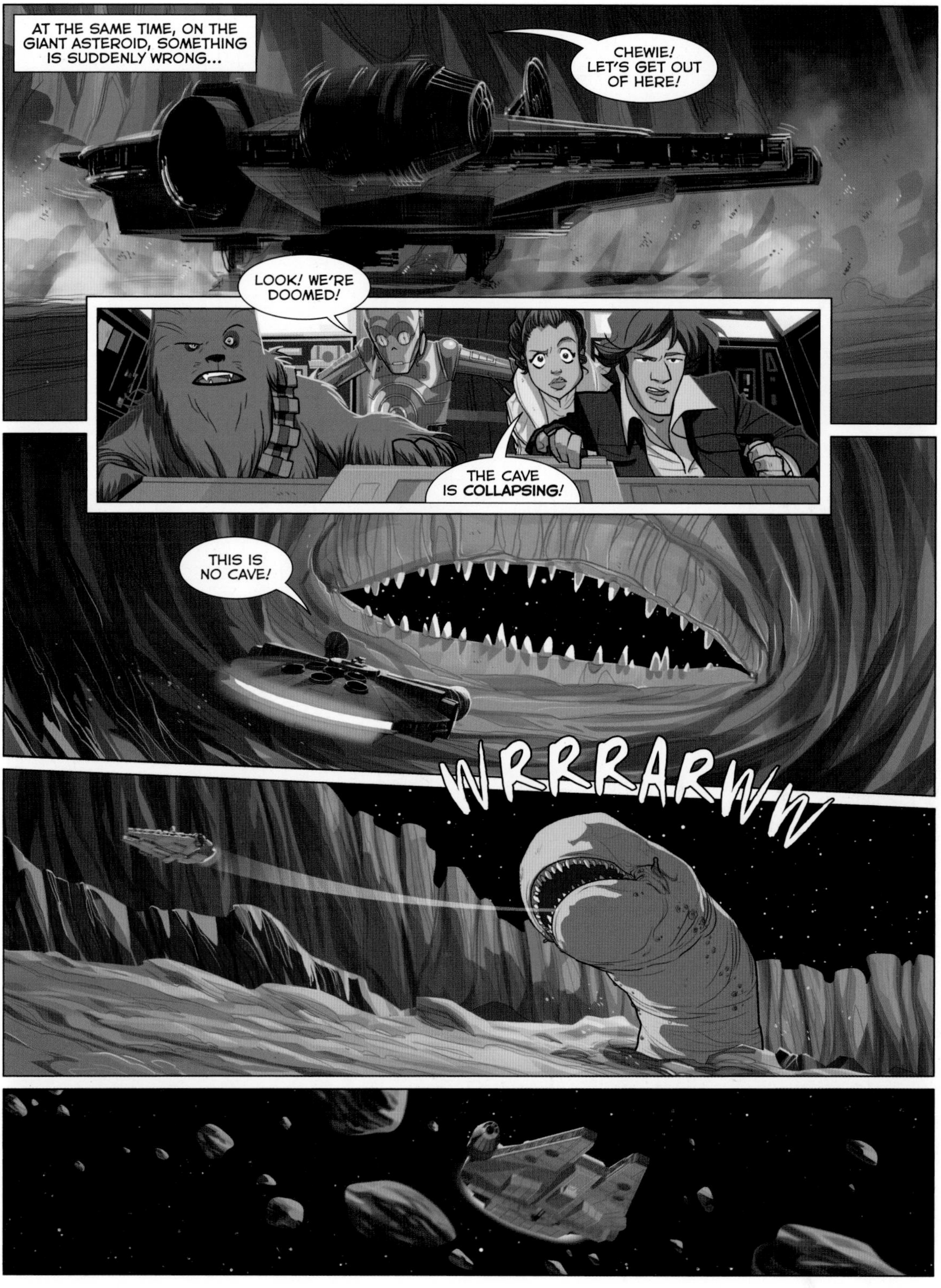
AT THE SAME TIME, ON THE GIANT ASTEROID, SOMETHING IS SUDDENLY WRONG...
CHEWIE! LET'S GET OUT OF HERE!
LOOK! WE'RE DOOMED!
THE CAVE IS COLLAPSING!
THIS IS NO CAVE!
WRRRARWN

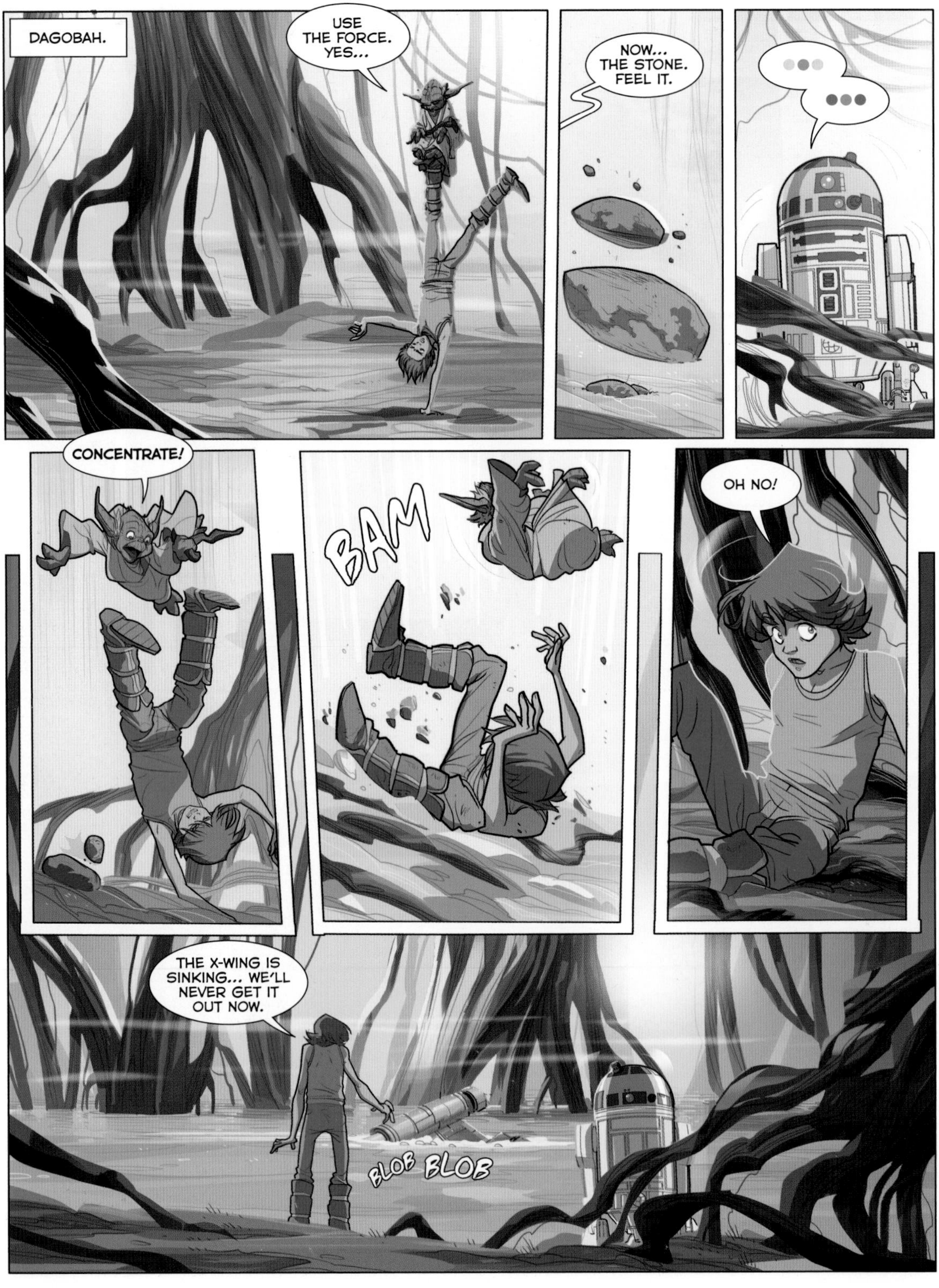
DAGOBAH.
USE THE FORCE. YES...
NOW... THE STONE. FEEL IT.
•••
•••
CONCENTRATE!
BAM
OH NO!
THE X-WING IS SINKING... WE'LL NEVER GET IT OUT NOW.
BLOB BLOB

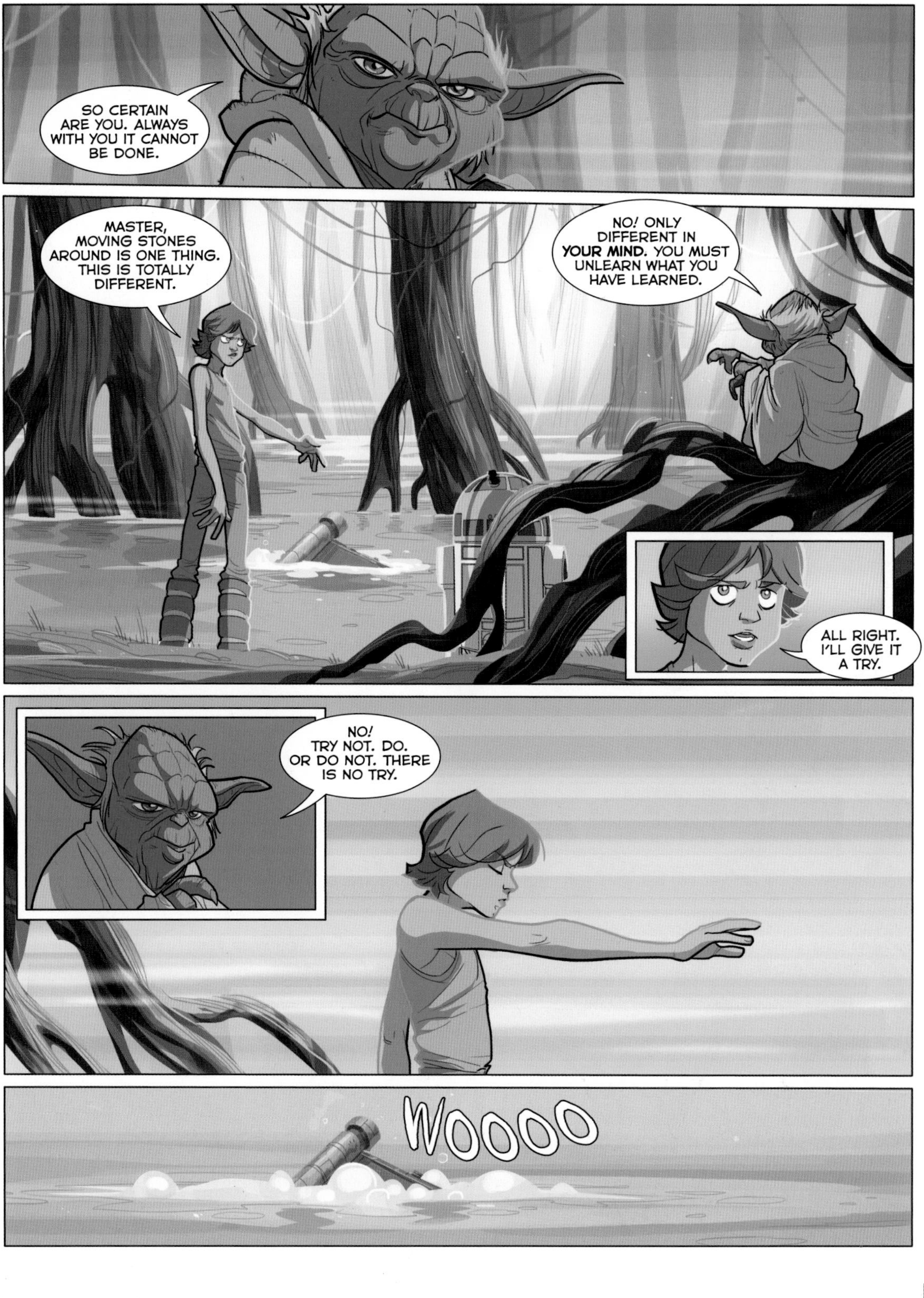
SO CERTAIN ARE YOU. ALWAYS WITH YOU IT CANNOT BE DONE.
MASTER, MOVING STONES AROUND IS ONE THING. THIS IS TOTALLY DIFFERENT.
NO! ONLY DIFFERENT IN YOUR MIND. YOU MUST UNLEARN WHAT YOU HAVE LEARNED.
ALL RIGHT. I'LL GIVE IT A TRY.
NO! TRY NOT. DO. OR DO NOT. THERE IS NO TRY.
WOOOO

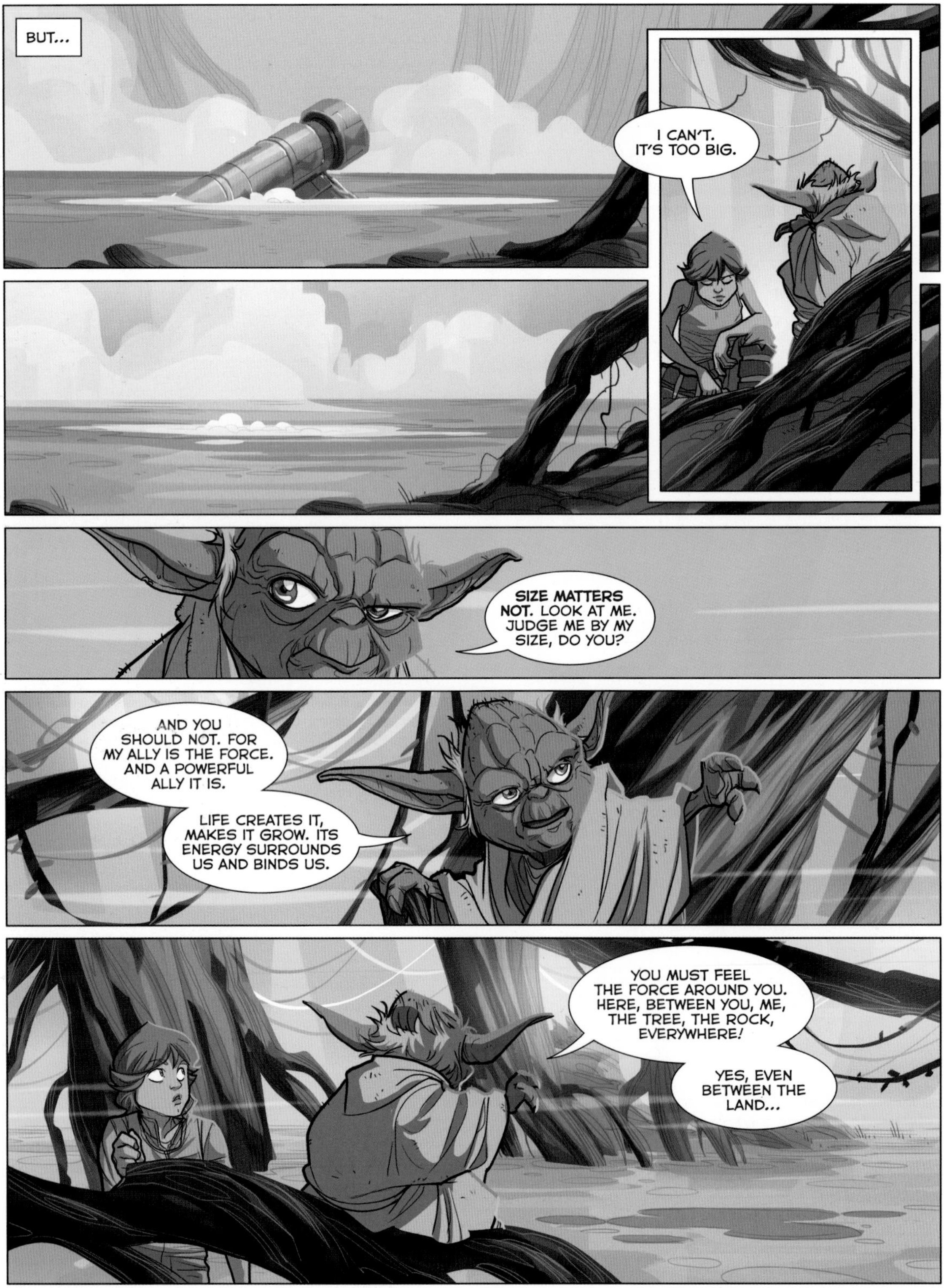
BUT...
I CAN'T. IT'S TOO BIG.
SIZE MATTERS NOT. LOOK AT ME. JUDGE ME BY MY SIZE, DO YOU?
AND YOU SHOULD NOT. FOR MY ALLY IS THE FORCE. AND A POWERFUL ALLY IT IS.
LIFE CREATES IT, MAKES IT GROW. ITS ENERGY SURROUNDS US AND BINDS US.
YOU MUST FEEL THE FORCE AROUND YOU. HERE, BETWEEN YOU, ME, THE TREE, THE ROCK, EVERYWHERE!
YES, EVEN BETWEEN THE LAND...

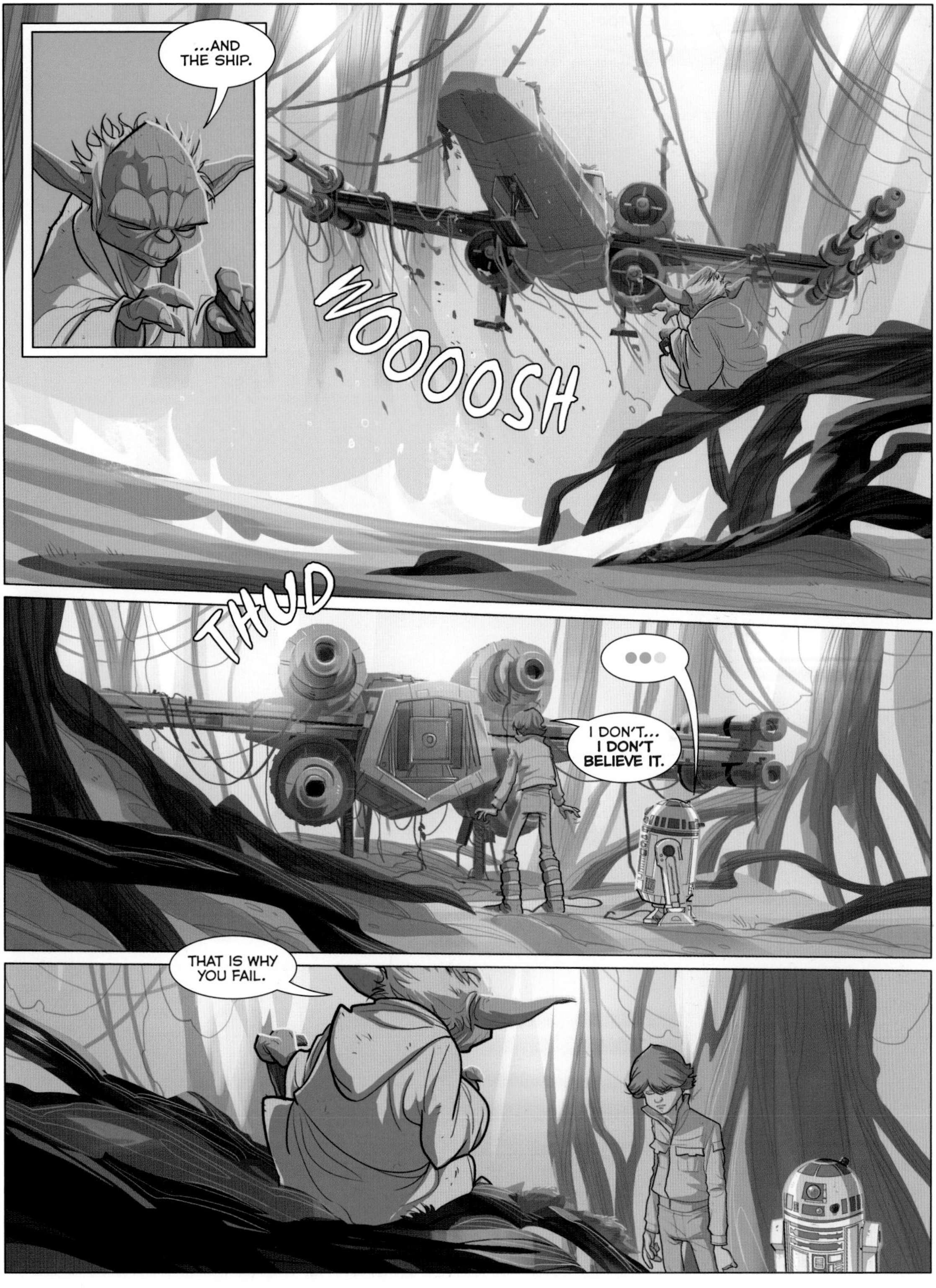
...AND THE SHIP.
WOOOOSH
THUD
I DON'T... I DON'T BELIEVE IT.
•••
THAT IS WHY YOU FAIL.

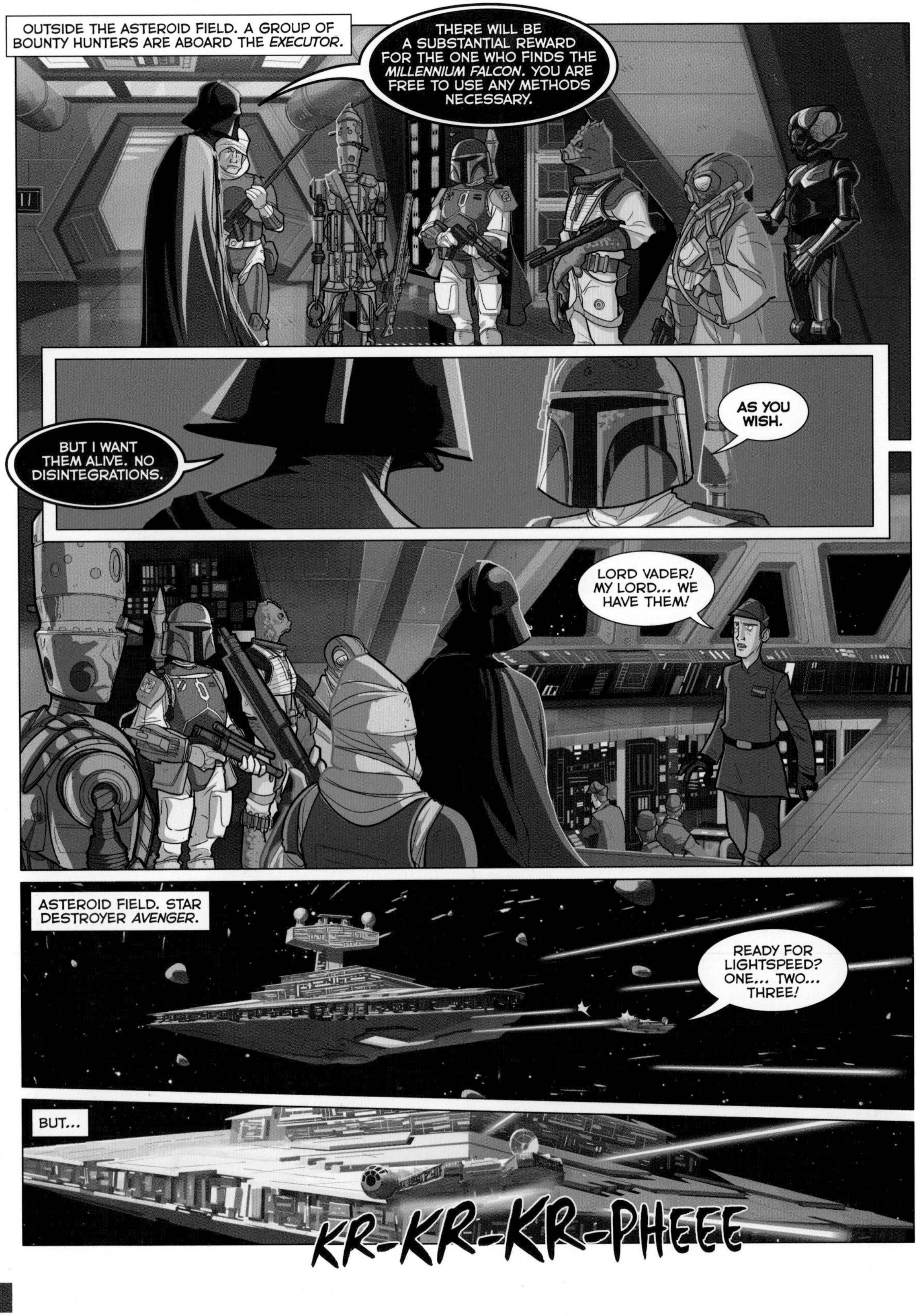
OUTSIDE THE ASTEROID FIELD. A GROUP OF BOUNTY HUNTERS ARE ABOARD THE *EXECUTOR*.
THERE WILL BE A SUBSTANTIAL REWARD FOR THE ONE WHO FINDS THE *MILLENNIUM FALCON*. YOU ARE FREE TO USE ANY METHODS NECESSARY.
BUT I WANT THEM ALIVE. NO DISINTEGRATIONS.
AS YOU WISH.
LORD VADER! MY LORD... WE HAVE THEM!
ASTEROID FIELD. STAR DESTROYER *AVENGER*.
READY FOR LIGHTSPEED? ONE... TWO... THREE!
BUT...
KR-KR-KR-PHEEE

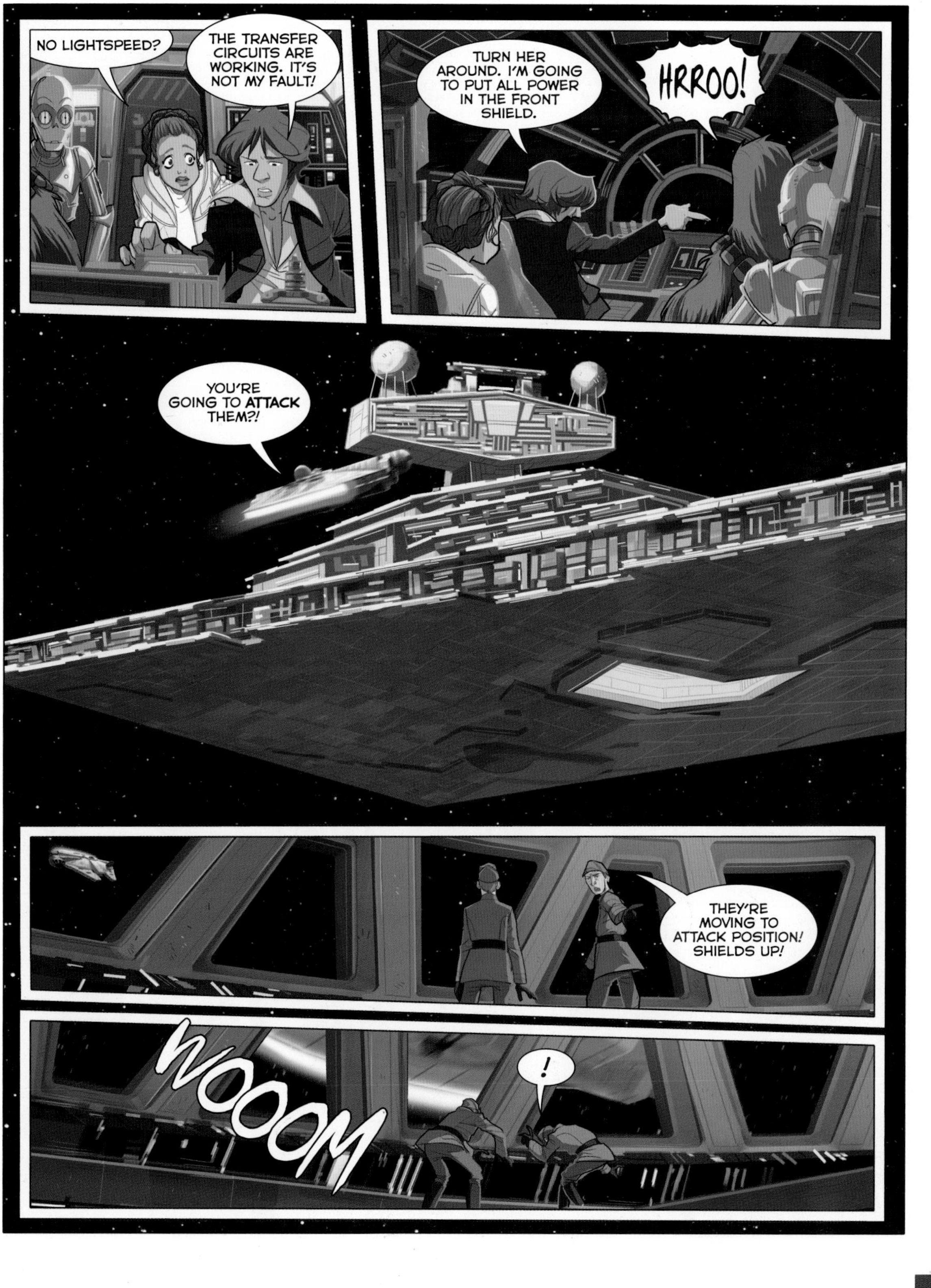
NO LIGHTSPEED?
THE TRANSFER CIRCUITS ARE WORKING. IT'S NOT MY FAULT!
TURN HER AROUND. I'M GOING TO PUT ALL POWER IN THE FRONT SHIELD.
HRROO!
YOU'RE GOING TO ATTACK THEM?!
THEY'RE MOVING TO ATTACK POSITION! SHIELDS UP!
WOOOM
!

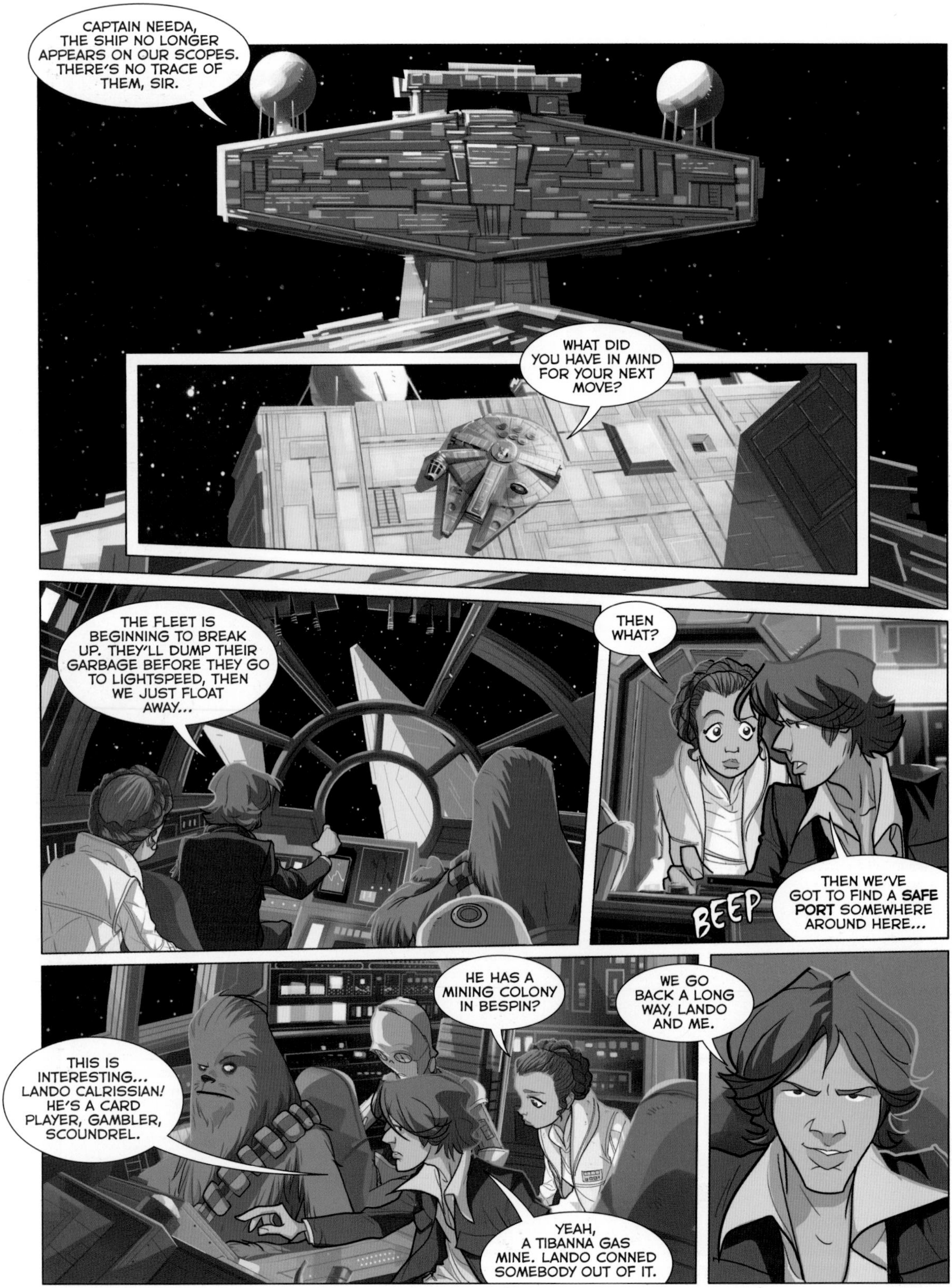
CAPTAIN NEEDA, THE SHIP NO LONGER APPEARS ON OUR SCOPES. THERE'S NO TRACE OF THEM, SIR.
WHAT DID YOU HAVE IN MIND FOR YOUR NEXT MOVE?
THE FLEET IS BEGINNING TO BREAK UP. THEY'LL DUMP THEIR GARBAGE BEFORE THEY GO TO LIGHTSPEED, THEN WE JUST FLOAT AWAY...
THEN WHAT?
THEN WE'VE GOT TO FIND A **SAFE PORT** SOMEWHERE AROUND HERE...
BEEP
THIS IS INTERESTING... LANDO CALRISSIAN! HE'S A CARD PLAYER, GAMBLER, SCOUNDREL.
HE HAS A MINING COLONY IN BESPIN?
YEAH, A TIBANNA GAS MINE. LANDO CONNED SOMEBODY OUT OF IT.
WE GO BACK A LONG WAY, LANDO AND ME.

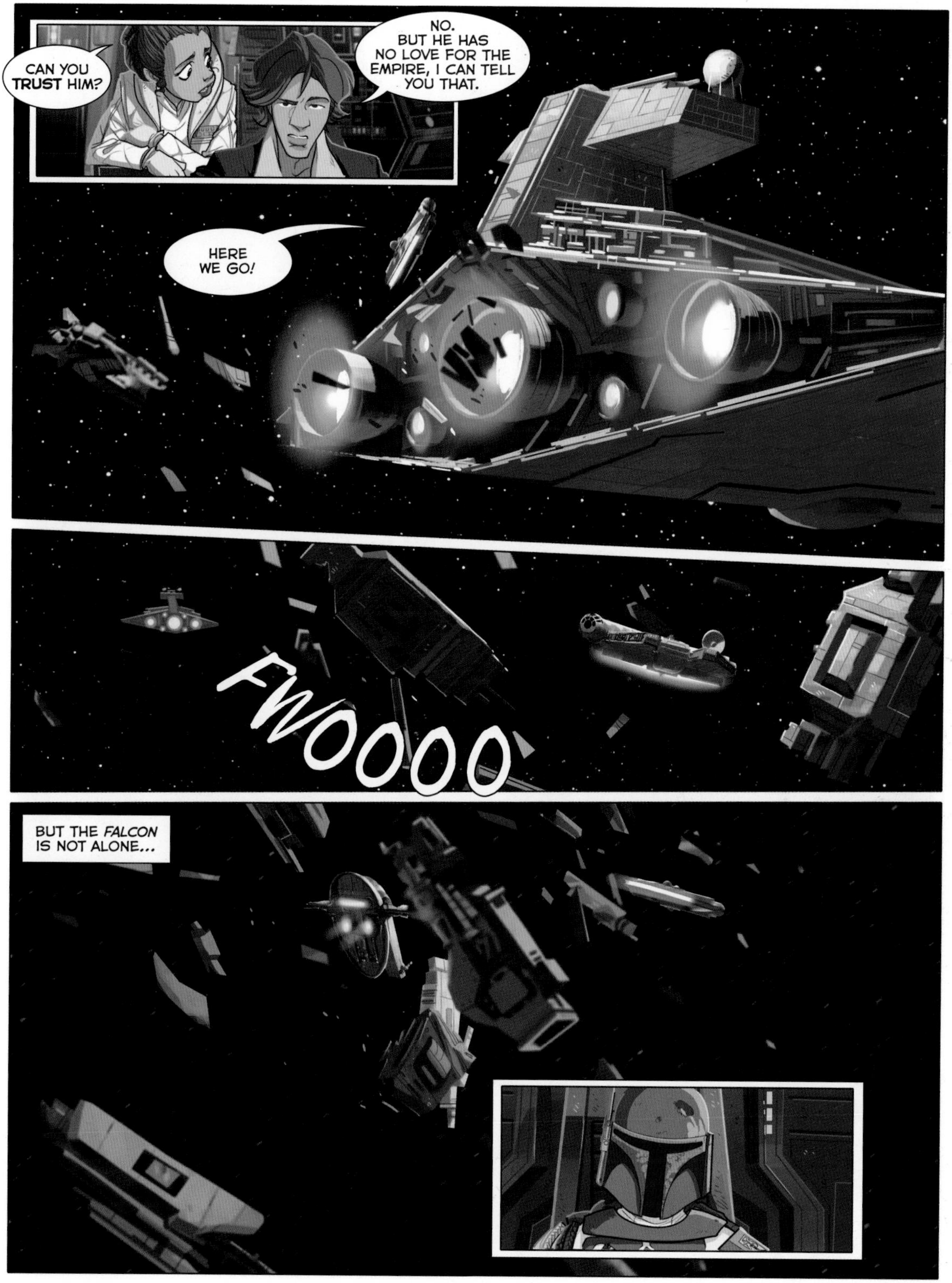
CAN YOU **TRUST** HIM?
NO. BUT HE HAS NO LOVE FOR THE EMPIRE, I CAN TELL YOU THAT.
HERE WE GO!
FWOOOO
BUT THE *FALCON* IS NOT ALONE...

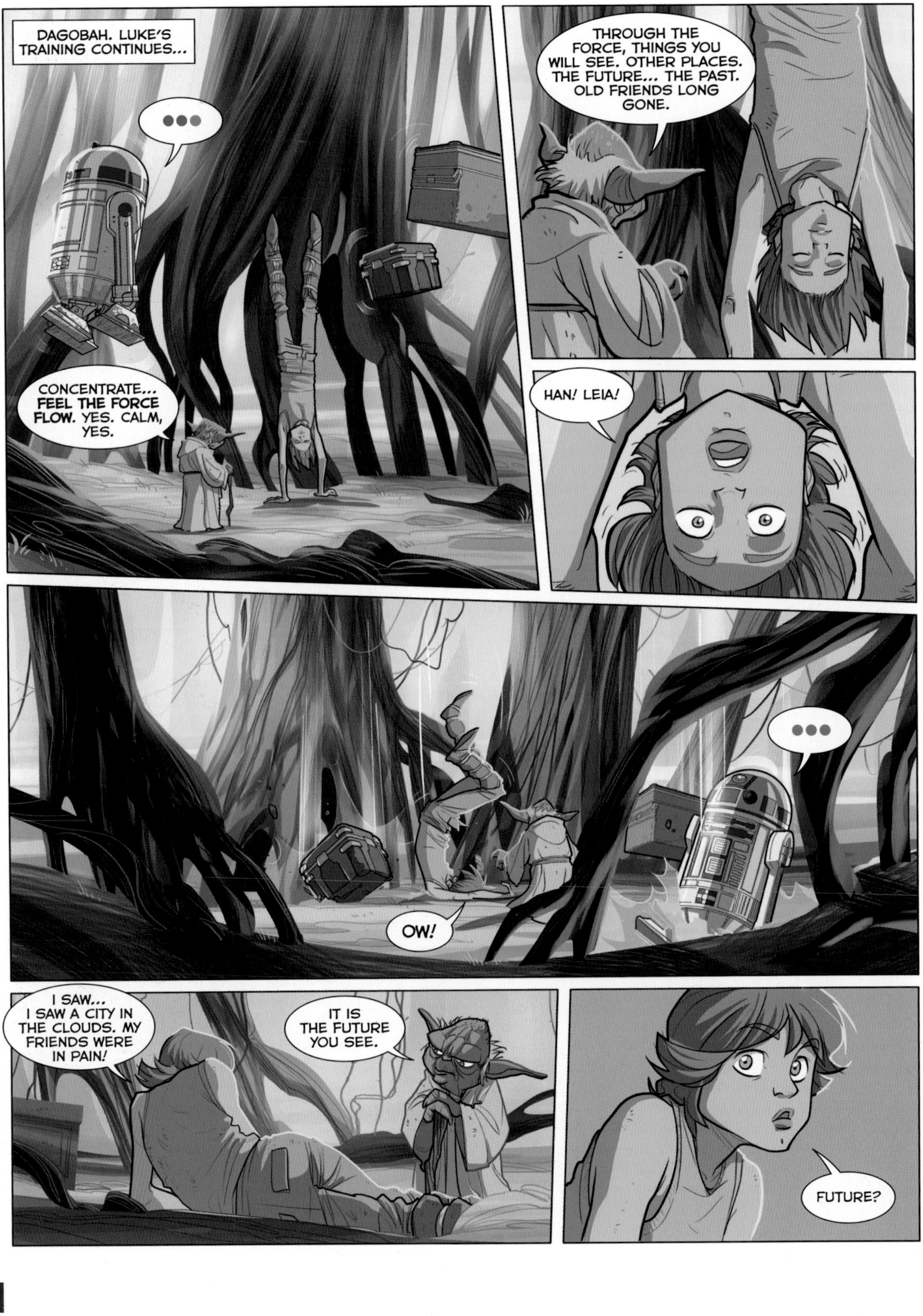

DAGOBAH. LUKE'S TRAINING CONTINUES...
•••
CONCENTRATE... **FEEL THE FORCE FLOW.** YES. CALM, YES.
THROUGH THE FORCE, THINGS YOU WILL SEE. OTHER PLACES. THE FUTURE... THE PAST. OLD FRIENDS LONG GONE.
HAN! LEIA!
•••
OW!
I SAW... I SAW A CITY IN THE CLOUDS. MY FRIENDS WERE IN PAIN!
IT IS THE FUTURE YOU SEE.
FUTURE?

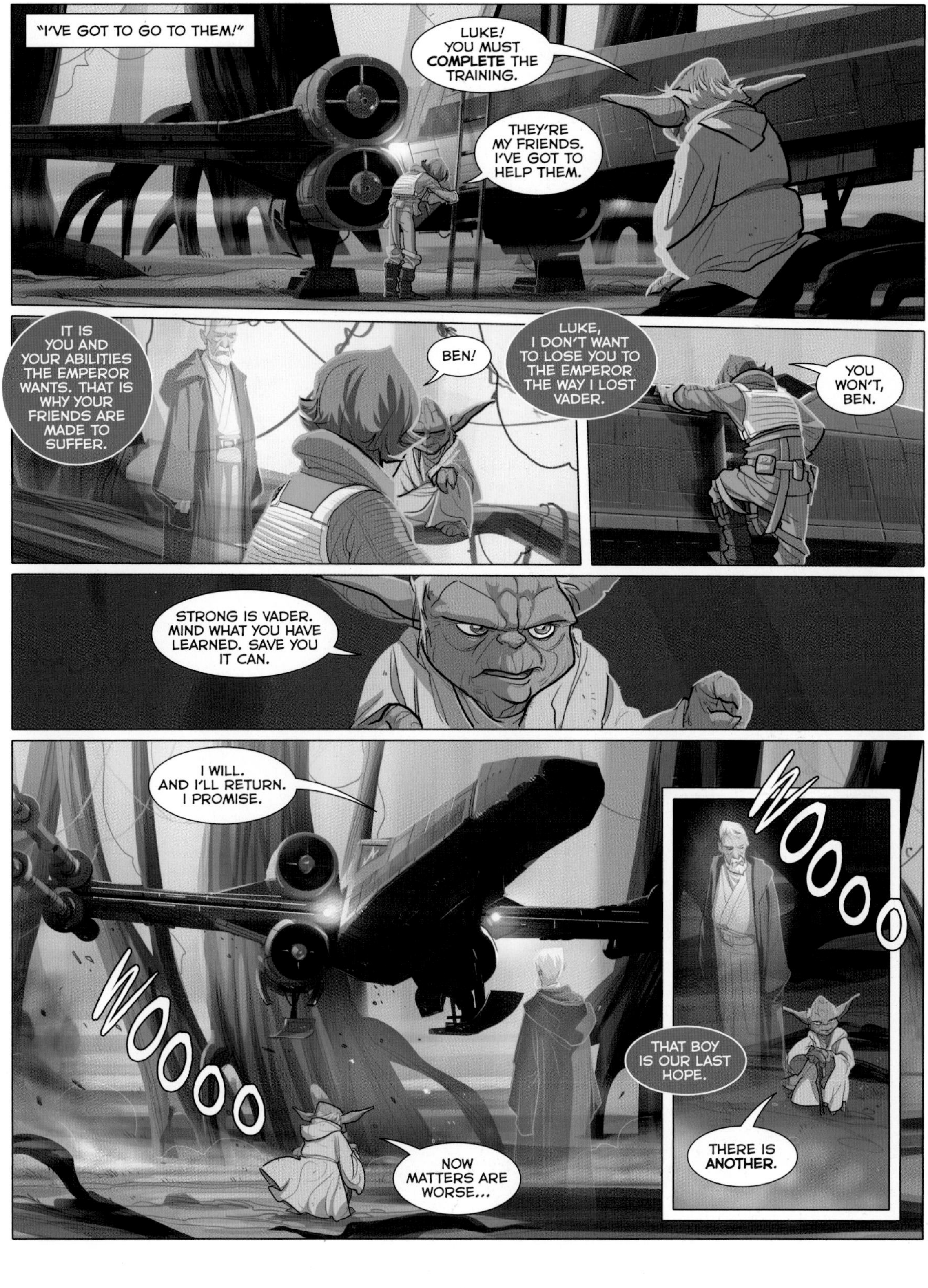

"I'VE GOT TO GO TO THEM!"
LUKE! YOU MUST COMPLETE THE TRAINING.
THEY'RE MY FRIENDS. I'VE GOT TO HELP THEM.
IT IS YOU AND YOUR ABILITIES THE EMPEROR WANTS. THAT IS WHY YOUR FRIENDS ARE MADE TO SUFFER.
BEN!
LUKE, I DON'T WANT TO LOSE YOU TO THE EMPEROR THE WAY I LOST VADER.
YOU WON'T, BEN.
STRONG IS VADER. MIND WHAT YOU HAVE LEARNED. SAVE YOU IT CAN.
I WILL. AND I'LL RETURN. I PROMISE.
WOOOO
WOOOO
NOW MATTERS ARE WORSE...
THAT BOY IS OUR LAST HOPE.
THERE IS ANOTHER.

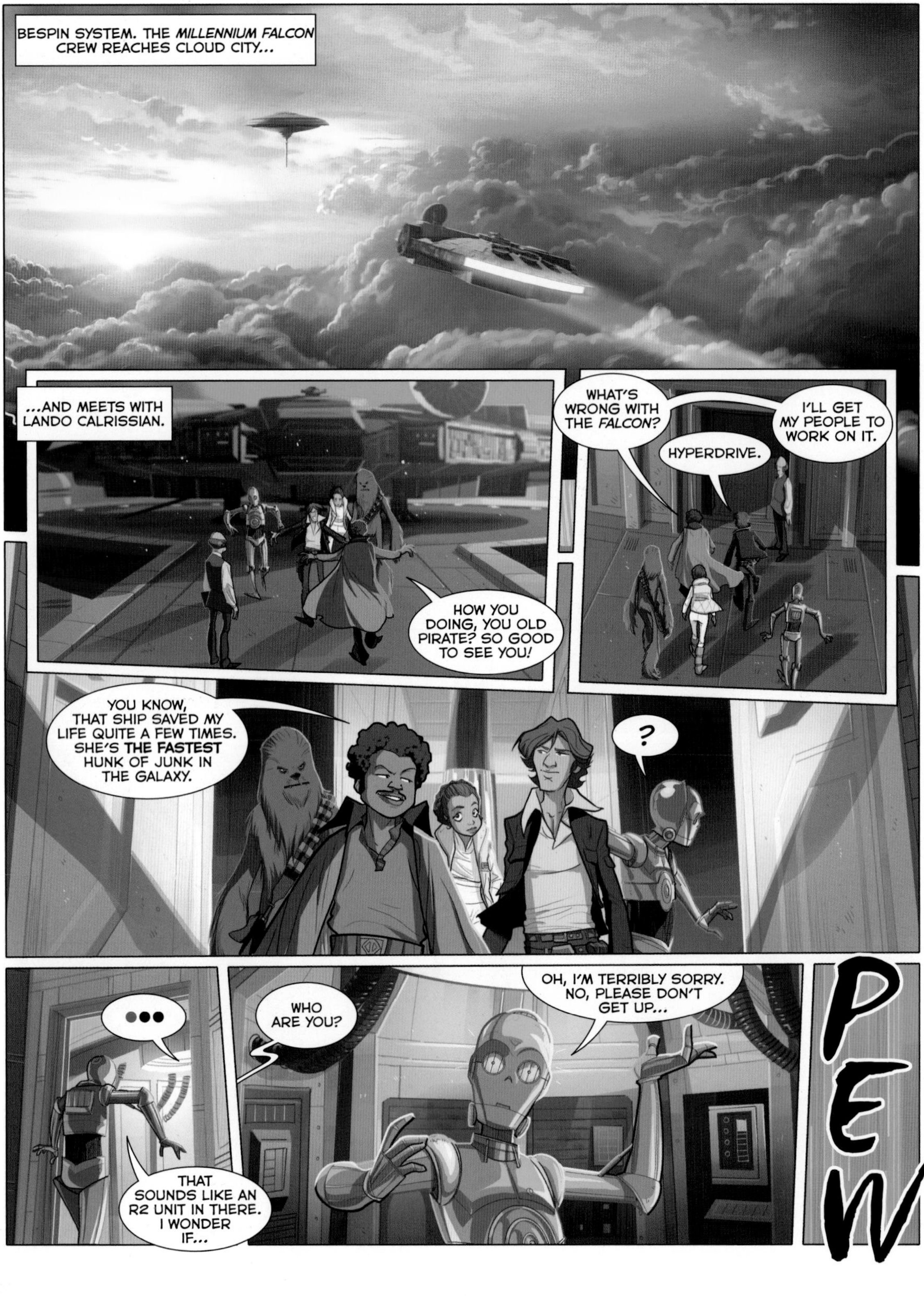
BESPIN SYSTEM. THE MILLENNIUM FALCON CREW REACHES CLOUD CITY...
...AND MEETS WITH LANDO CALRISSIAN.
HOW YOU DOING, YOU OLD PIRATE? SO GOOD TO SEE YOU!
WHAT'S WRONG WITH THE FALCON?
HYPERDRIVE.
I'LL GET MY PEOPLE TO WORK ON IT.
YOU KNOW, THAT SHIP SAVED MY LIFE QUITE A FEW TIMES. SHE'S THE FASTEST HUNK OF JUNK IN THE GALAXY.
?
•••
THAT SOUNDS LIKE AN R2 UNIT IN THERE. I WONDER IF...
WHO ARE YOU?
OH, I'M TERRIBLY SORRY. NO, PLEASE DON'T GET UP...
PEW

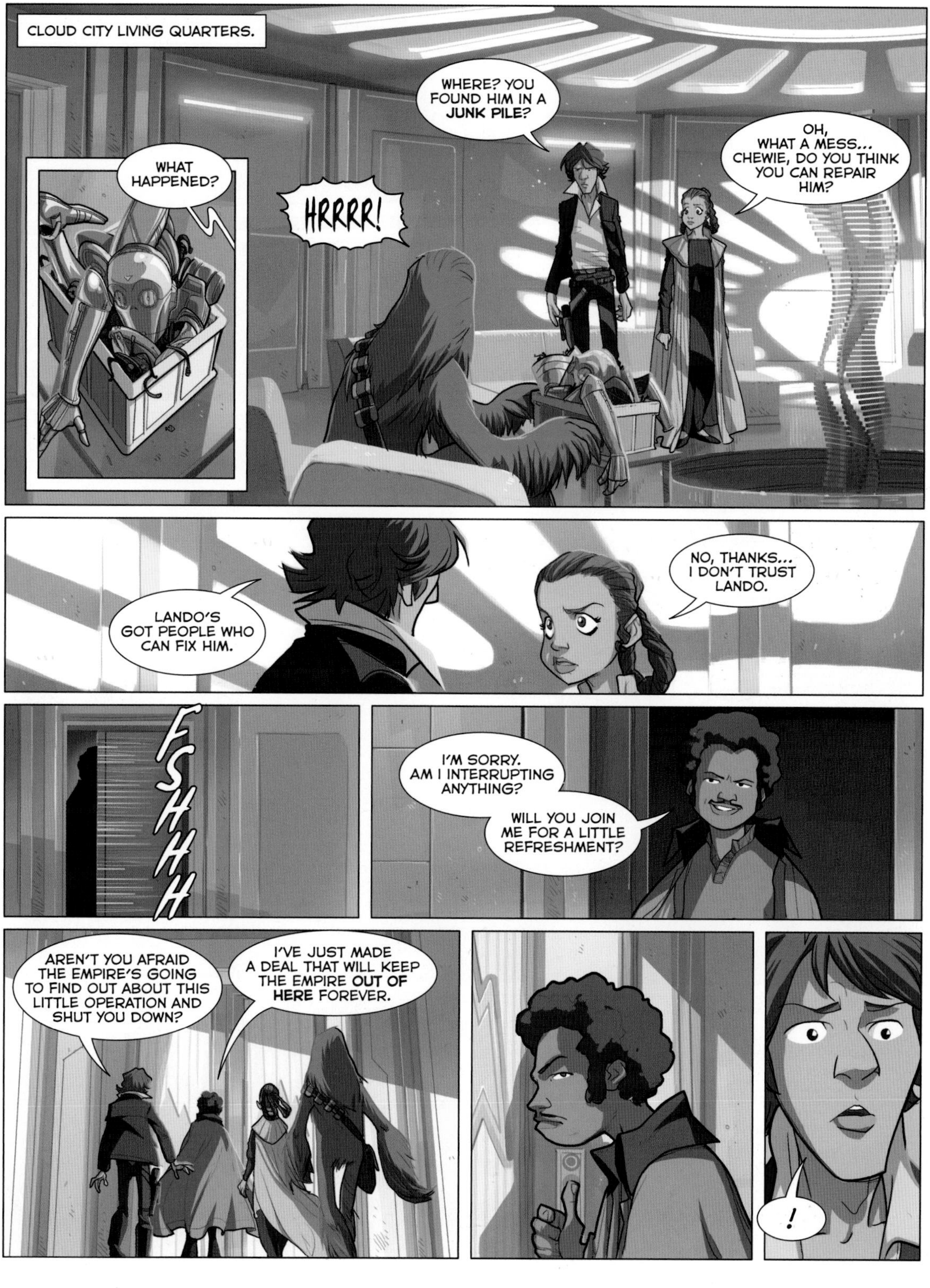
CLOUD CITY LIVING QUARTERS.
WHERE? YOU FOUND HIM IN A JUNK PILE?
OH, WHAT A MESS... CHEWIE, DO YOU THINK YOU CAN REPAIR HIM?
WHAT HAPPENED?
HRRRR!
LANDO'S GOT PEOPLE WHO CAN FIX HIM.
NO, THANKS... I DON'T TRUST LANDO.
FSHHH
I'M SORRY. AM I INTERRUPTING ANYTHING?
WILL YOU JOIN ME FOR A LITTLE REFRESHMENT?
AREN'T YOU AFRAID THE EMPIRE'S GOING TO FIND OUT ABOUT THIS LITTLE OPERATION AND SHUT YOU DOWN?
I'VE JUST MADE A DEAL THAT WILL KEEP THE EMPIRE OUT OF HERE FOREVER.
!

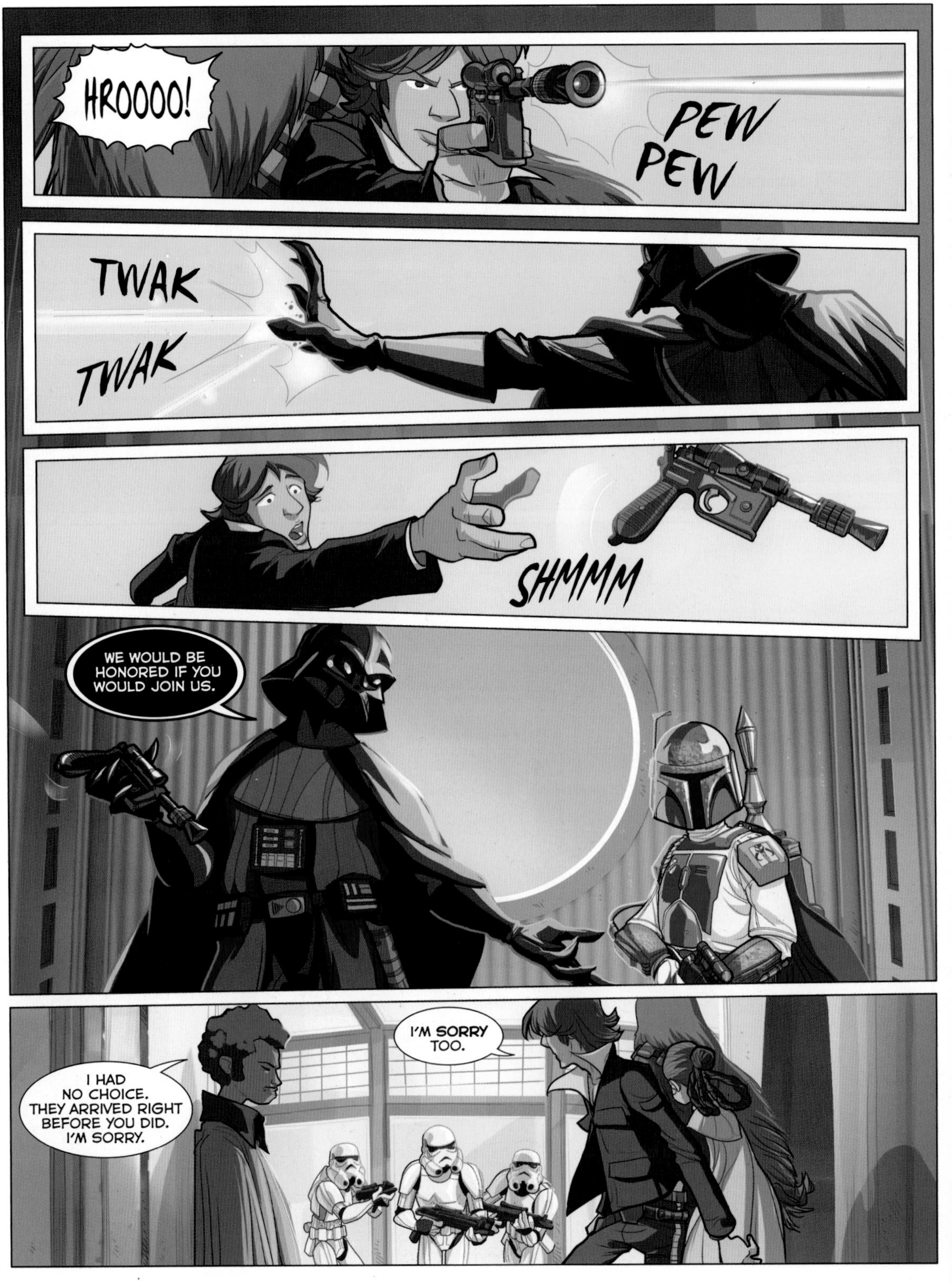
HROOOO!
PEW PEW
TWAK
TWAK
SHMMM
WE WOULD BE HONORED IF YOU WOULD JOIN US.
I HAD NO CHOICE. THEY ARRIVED RIGHT BEFORE YOU DID. I'M SORRY.
I'M SORRY TOO.

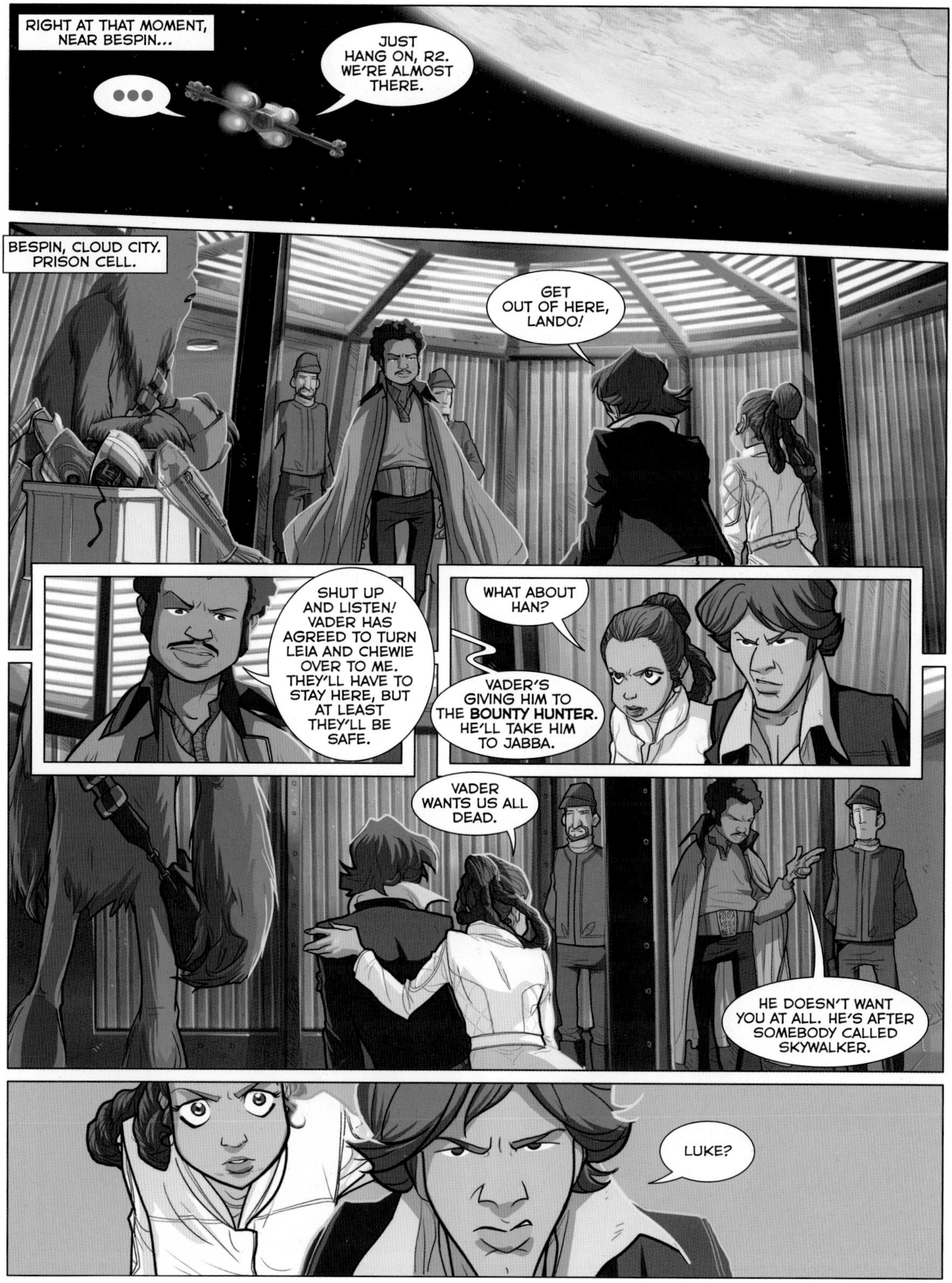
RIGHT AT THAT MOMENT, NEAR BESPIN...
•••
JUST HANG ON, R2. WE'RE ALMOST THERE.
BESPIN, CLOUD CITY. PRISON CELL.
GET OUT OF HERE, LANDO!
SHUT UP AND LISTEN! VADER HAS AGREED TO TURN LEIA AND CHEWIE OVER TO ME. THEY'LL HAVE TO STAY HERE, BUT AT LEAST THEY'LL BE SAFE.
WHAT ABOUT HAN?
VADER'S GIVING HIM TO THE **BOUNTY HUNTER**. HE'LL TAKE HIM TO JABBA.
VADER WANTS US ALL DEAD.
HE DOESN'T WANT YOU AT ALL. HE'S AFTER SOMEBODY CALLED SKYWALKER.
LUKE?

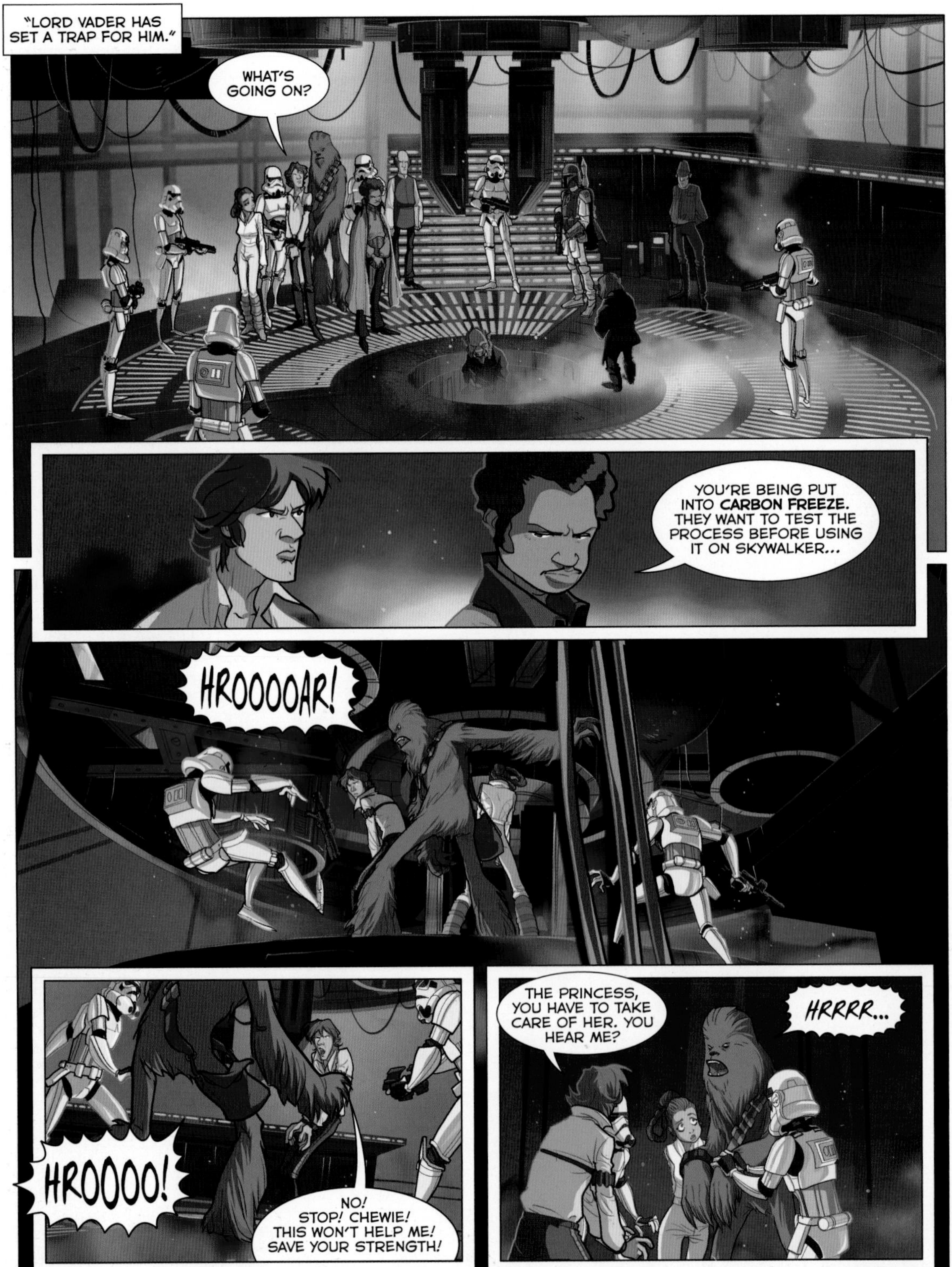
"LORD VADER HAS SET A TRAP FOR HIM."
WHAT'S GOING ON?
YOU'RE BEING PUT INTO **CARBON FREEZE.** THEY WANT TO TEST THE PROCESS BEFORE USING IT ON SKYWALKER...
HROOOOAR!
HROOOO!
NO! STOP! CHEWIE! THIS WON'T HELP ME! SAVE YOUR STRENGTH!
THE PRINCESS, YOU HAVE TO TAKE CARE OF HER. YOU HEAR ME?
HRRRR...

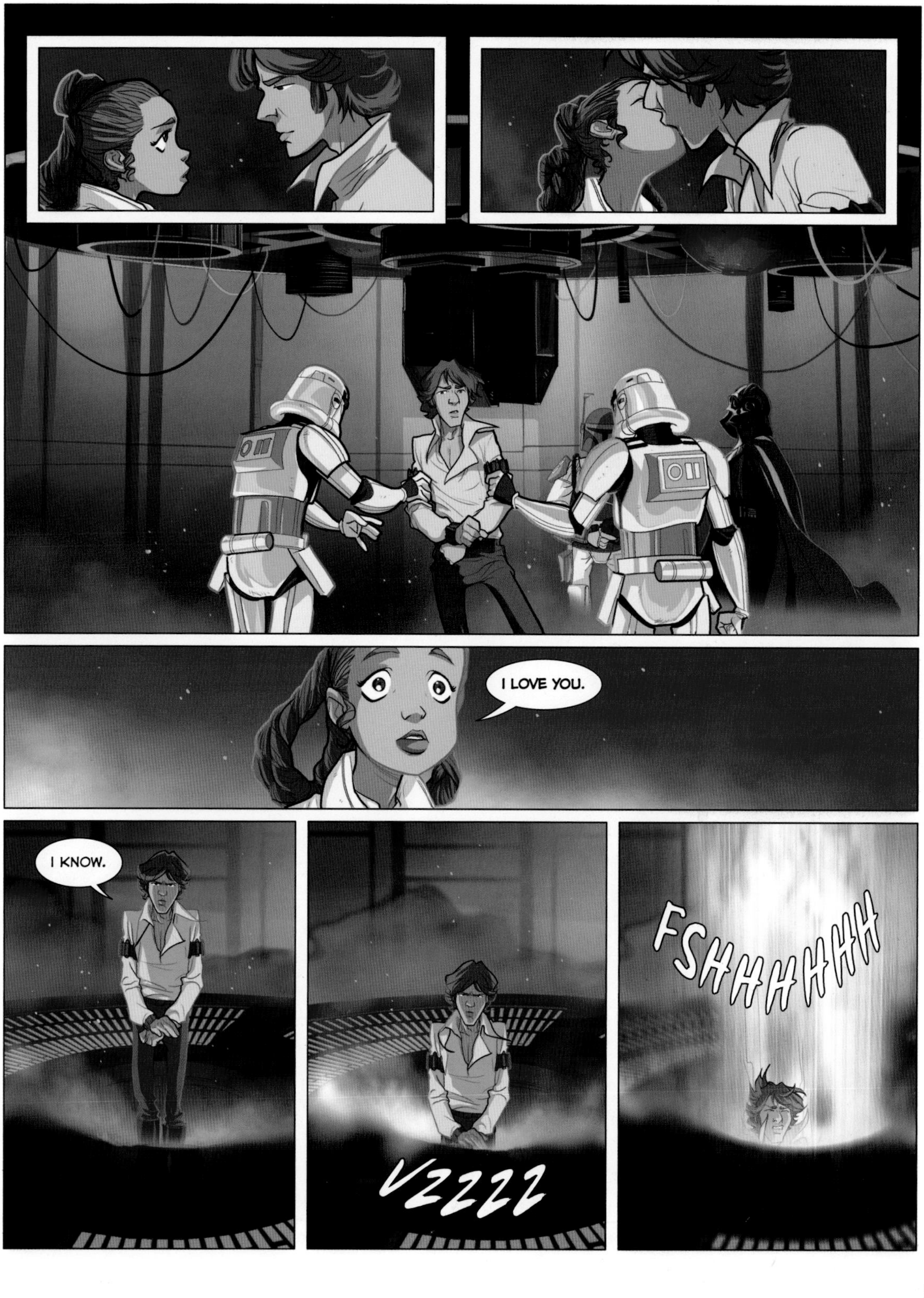
I LOVE YOU.
I KNOW.
VZZZZ
FSHHHHHH

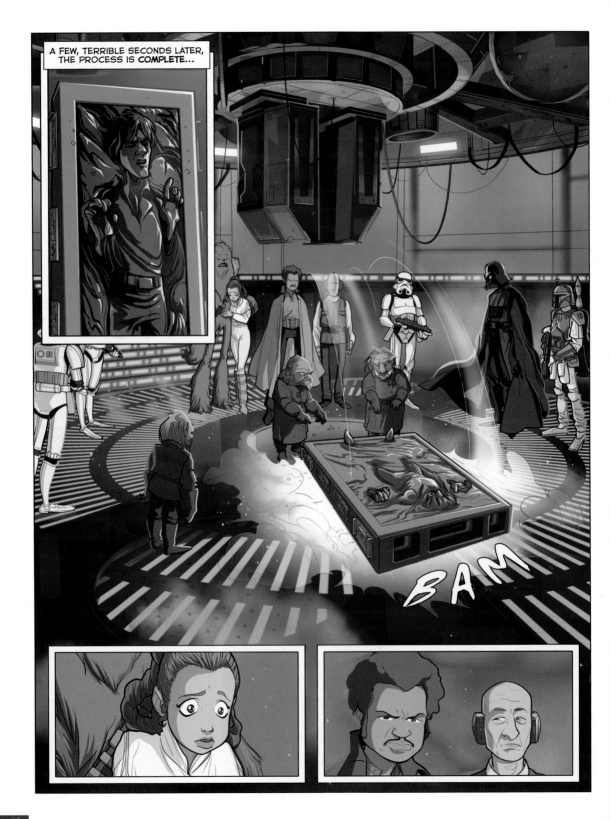

A FEW, TERRIBLE SECONDS LATER, THE PROCESS IS **COMPLETE**...

BAM

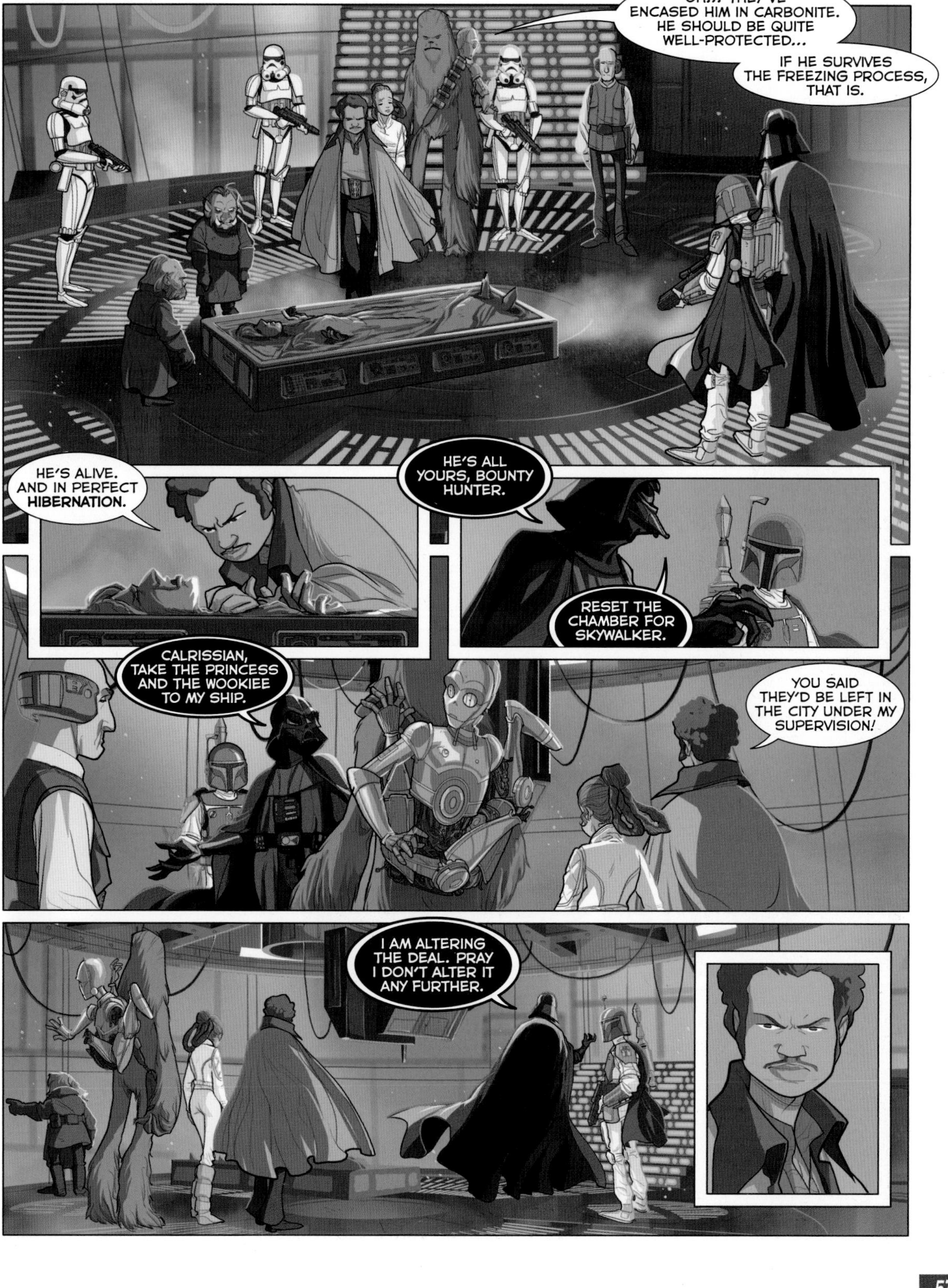
OH... THEY'VE ENCASED HIM IN CARBONITE. HE SHOULD BE QUITE WELL-PROTECTED...
IF HE SURVIVES THE FREEZING PROCESS, THAT IS.
HE'S ALIVE. AND IN PERFECT HIBERNATION.
HE'S ALL YOURS, BOUNTY HUNTER.
RESET THE CHAMBER FOR SKYWALKER.
CALRISSIAN, TAKE THE PRINCESS AND THE WOOKIEE TO MY SHIP.
YOU SAID THEY'D BE LEFT IN THE CITY UNDER MY SUPERVISION!
I AM ALTERING THE DEAL. PRAY I DON'T ALTER IT ANY FURTHER.

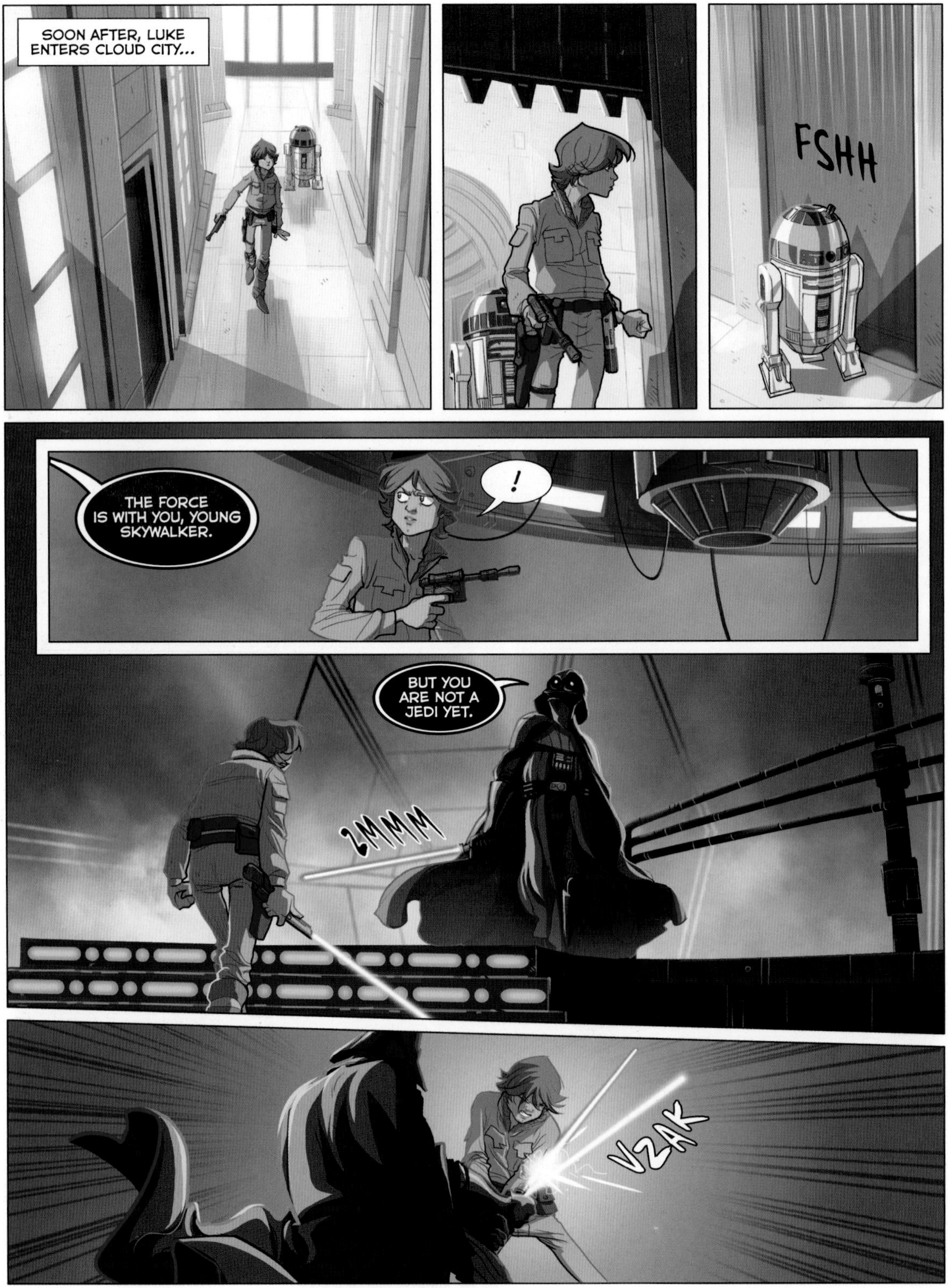
SOON AFTER, LUKE ENTERS CLOUD CITY...
FSHH
THE FORCE IS WITH YOU, YOUNG SKYWALKER.
!
BUT YOU ARE NOT A JEDI YET.
ZMMM
VZAK

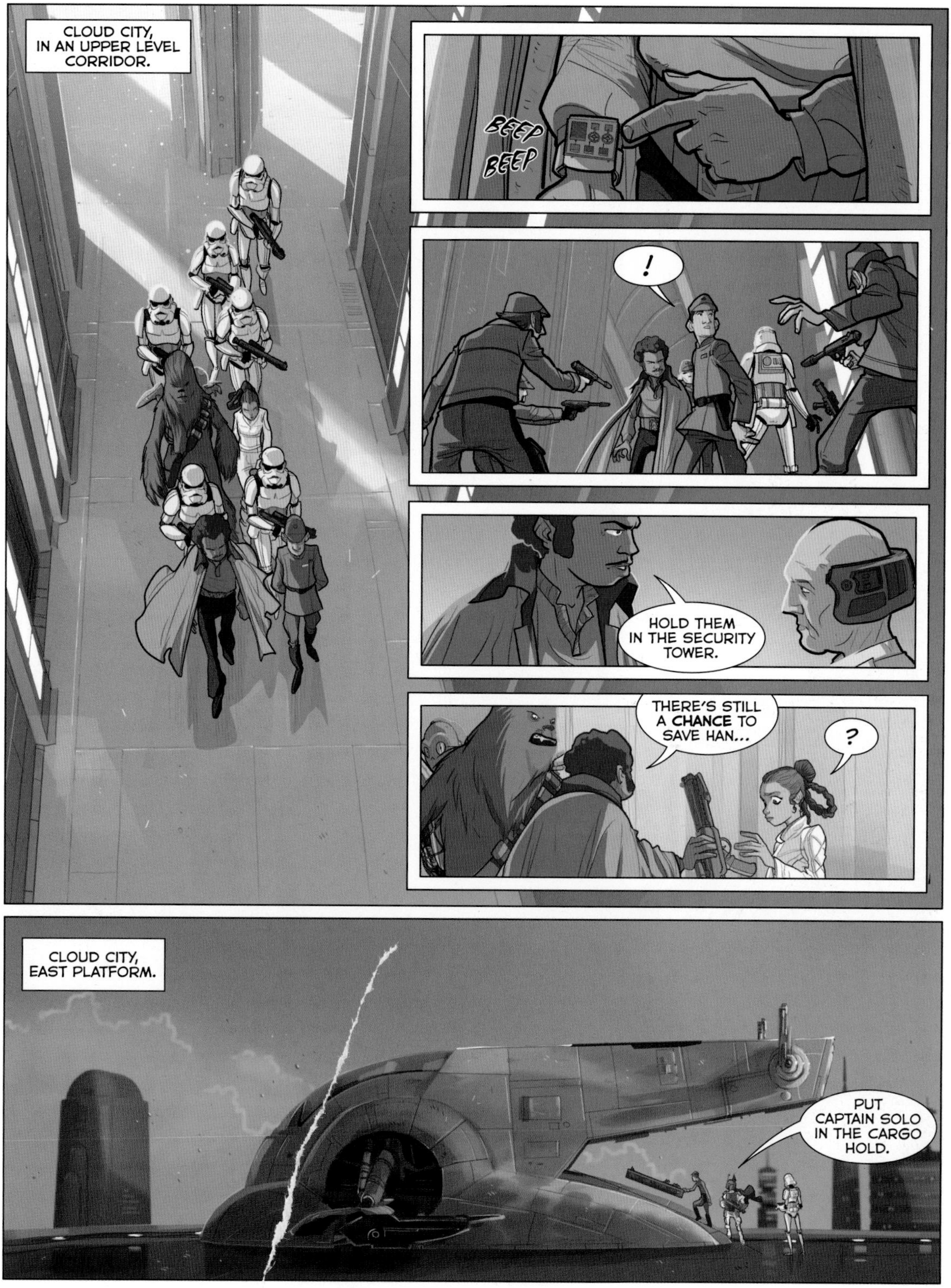
CLOUD CITY, IN AN UPPER LEVEL CORRIDOR.
BEEP BEEP
!
HOLD THEM IN THE SECURITY TOWER.
THERE'S STILL A CHANCE TO SAVE HAN...
?
CLOUD CITY, EAST PLATFORM.
PUT CAPTAIN SOLO IN THE CARGO HOLD.

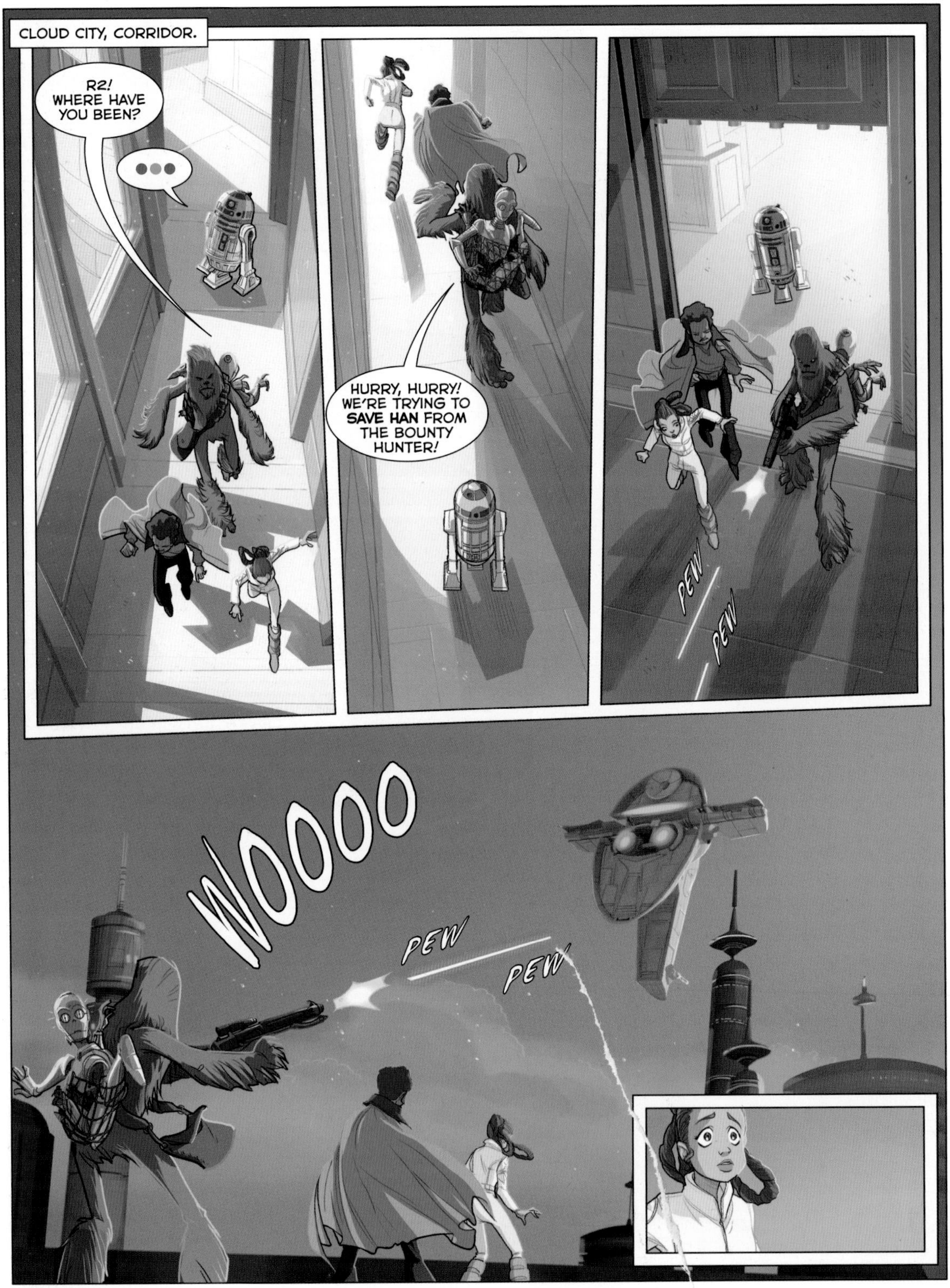
CLOUD CITY, CORRIDOR.
R2! WHERE HAVE YOU BEEN?
HURRY, HURRY! WE'RE TRYING TO SAVE HAN FROM THE BOUNTY HUNTER!
PEW
PEW
WOOOO
PEW
PEW

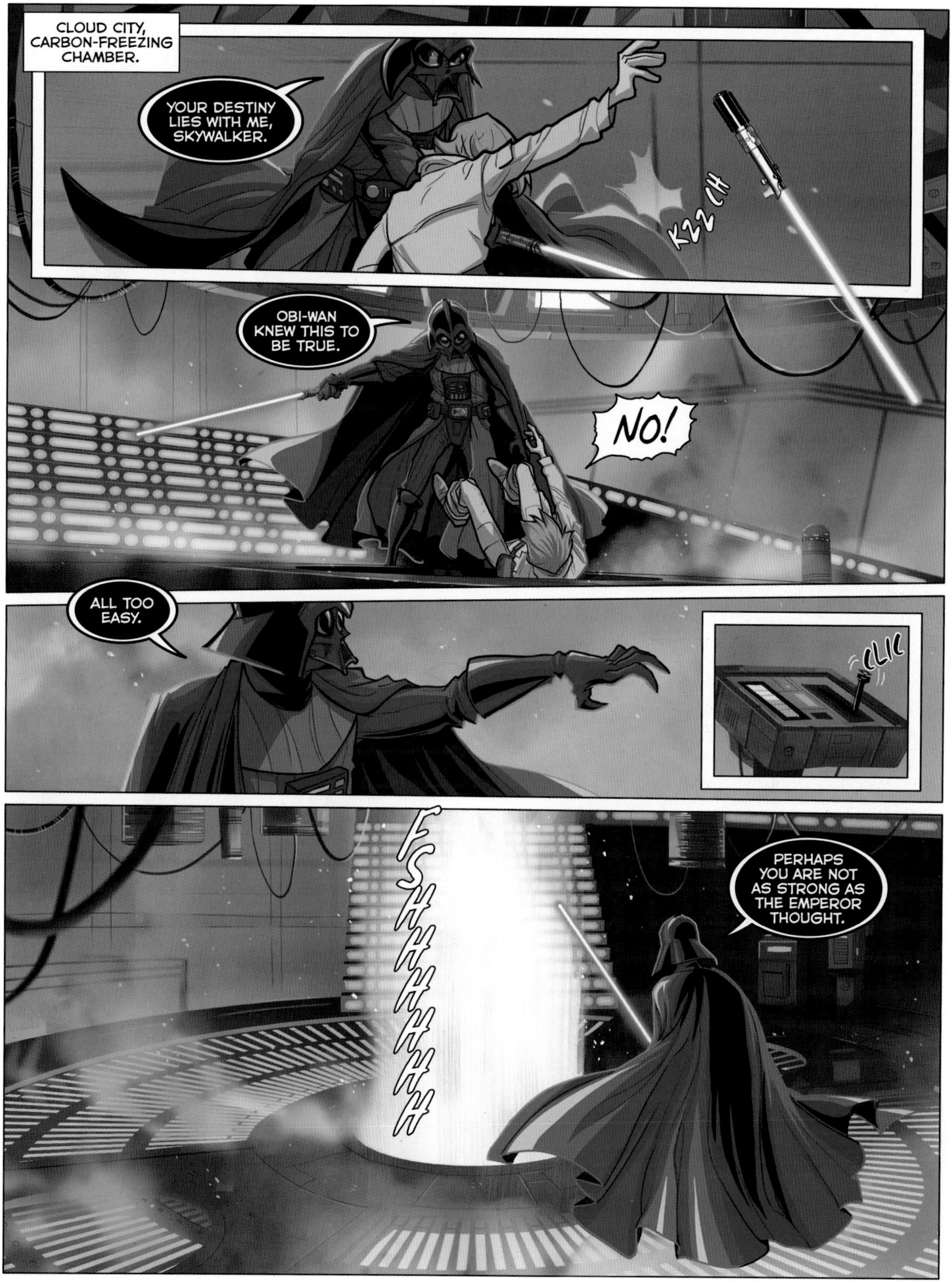
CLOUD CITY, CARBON-FREEZING CHAMBER.
YOUR DESTINY LIES WITH ME, SKYWALKER.
KZZ CH
OBI-WAN KNEW THIS TO BE TRUE.
NO!
ALL TOO EASY.
CLIC
FSHHHHHHHHH
PERHAPS YOU ARE NOT AS STRONG AS THE EMPEROR THOUGHT.

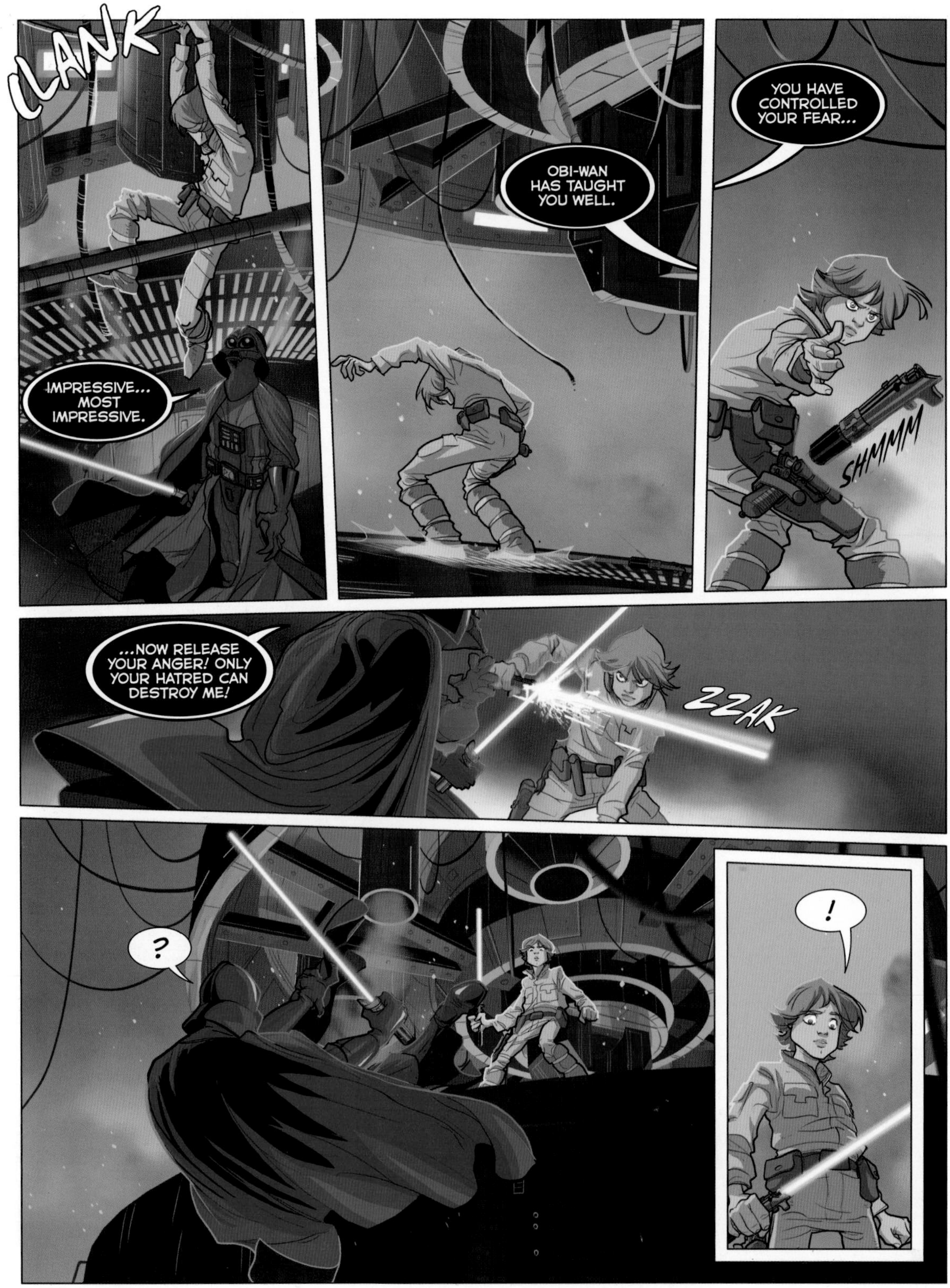
CLANK
IMPRESSIVE... MOST IMPRESSIVE.
OBI-WAN HAS TAUGHT YOU WELL.
YOU HAVE CONTROLLED YOUR FEAR...
SHMMM
...NOW RELEASE YOUR ANGER! ONLY YOUR HATRED CAN DESTROY ME!
ZZAK
?
!

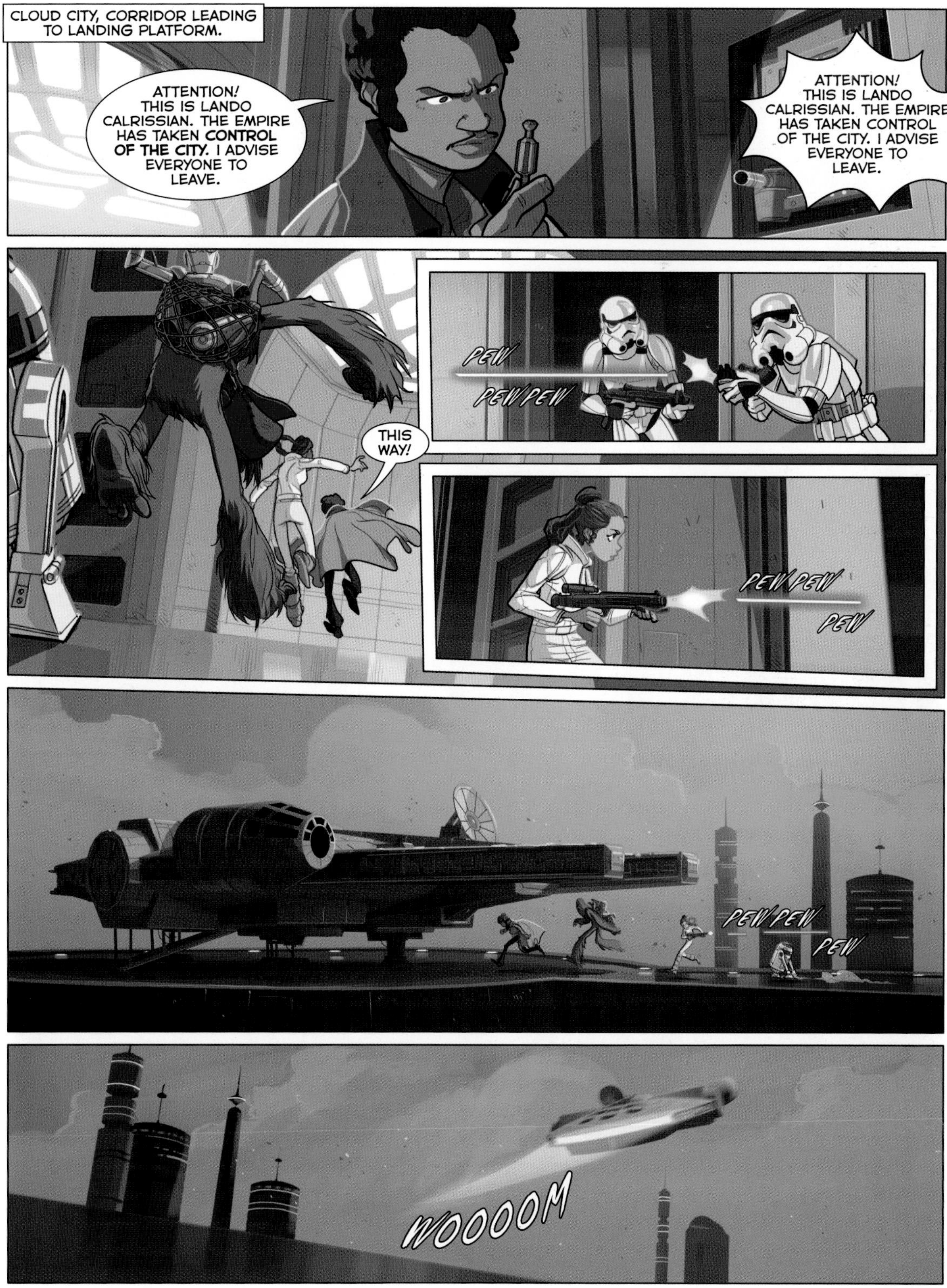

CLOUD CITY, CORRIDOR LEADING TO LANDING PLATFORM.
ATTENTION! THIS IS LANDO CALRISSIAN. THE EMPIRE HAS TAKEN **CONTROL OF THE CITY**. I ADVISE EVERYONE TO LEAVE.
ATTENTION! THIS IS LANDO CALRISSIAN. THE EMPIRE HAS TAKEN CONTROL OF THE CITY. I ADVISE EVERYONE TO LEAVE.
THIS WAY!
PEW
PEW PEW
PEW PEW
PEW
PEW PEW
PEW
WOOOOM

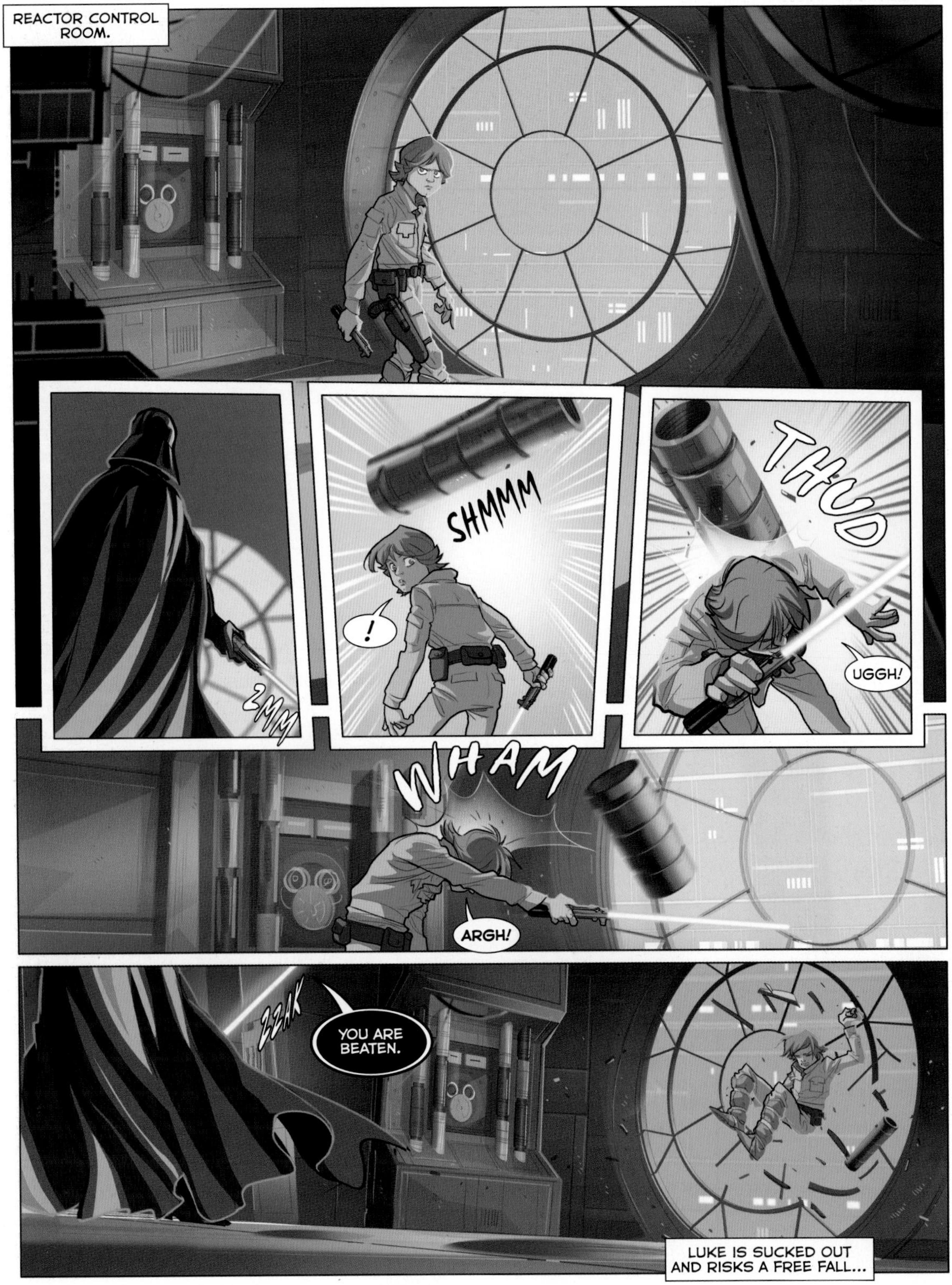
REACTOR CONTROL ROOM.
ZMM
SHMMM
!
THUD
UGGH!
WHAM
ARGH!
ZZAK
YOU ARE BEATEN.
LUKE IS SUCKED OUT AND RISKS A FREE FALL...

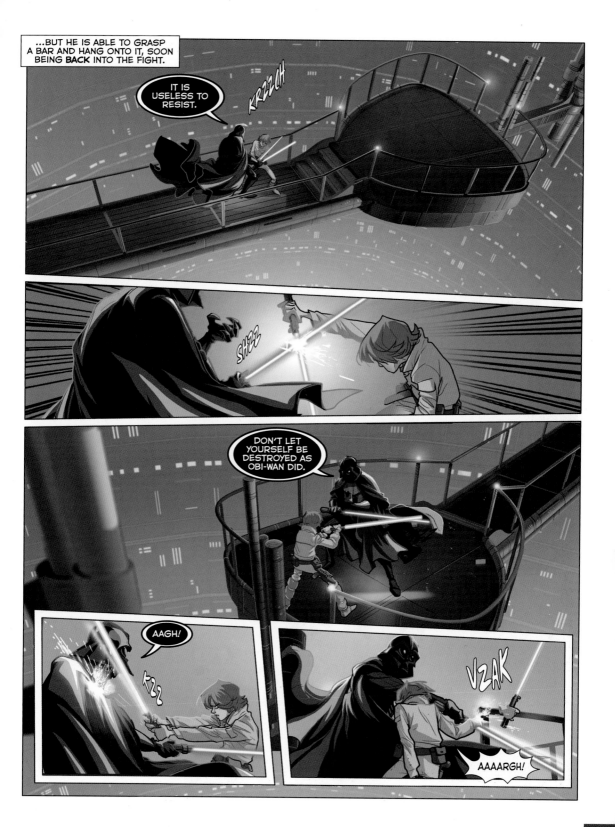

...BUT HE IS ABLE TO GRASP A BAR AND HANG ONTO IT, SOON BEING **BACK** INTO THE FIGHT.

IT IS USELESS TO RESIST.

KRZZCH

SHZZ

DON'T LET YOURSELF BE DESTROYED AS OBI-WAN DID.

AAGH!

KZZ

VZAK

AAAARGH!

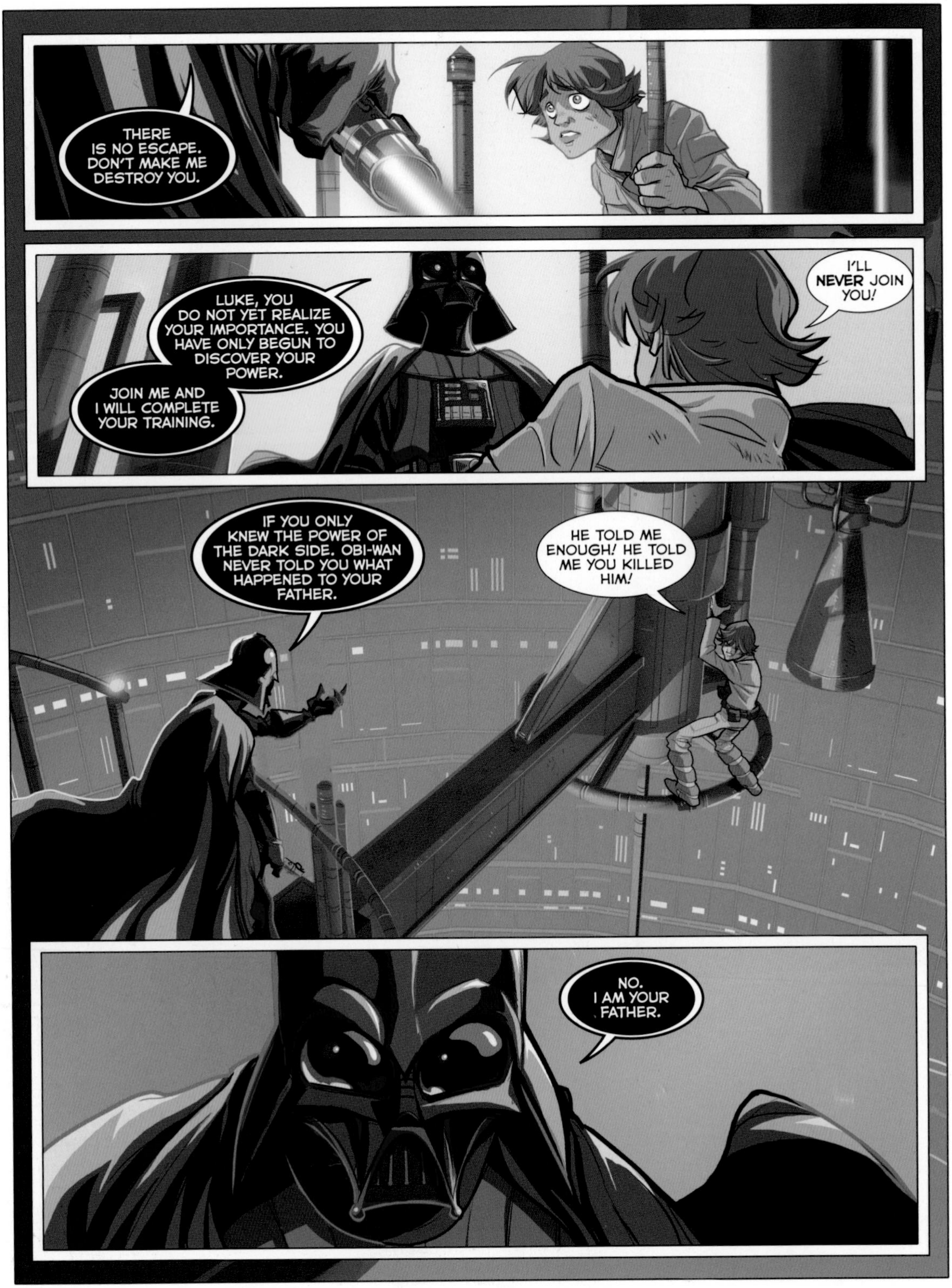
THERE IS NO ESCAPE. DON'T MAKE ME DESTROY YOU.
LUKE, YOU DO NOT YET REALIZE YOUR IMPORTANCE. YOU HAVE ONLY BEGUN TO DISCOVER YOUR POWER.
JOIN ME AND I WILL COMPLETE YOUR TRAINING.
I'LL **NEVER** JOIN YOU!
IF YOU ONLY KNEW THE POWER OF THE DARK SIDE. OBI-WAN NEVER TOLD YOU WHAT HAPPENED TO YOUR FATHER.
HE TOLD ME ENOUGH! HE TOLD ME YOU KILLED HIM!
NO. I AM YOUR FATHER.

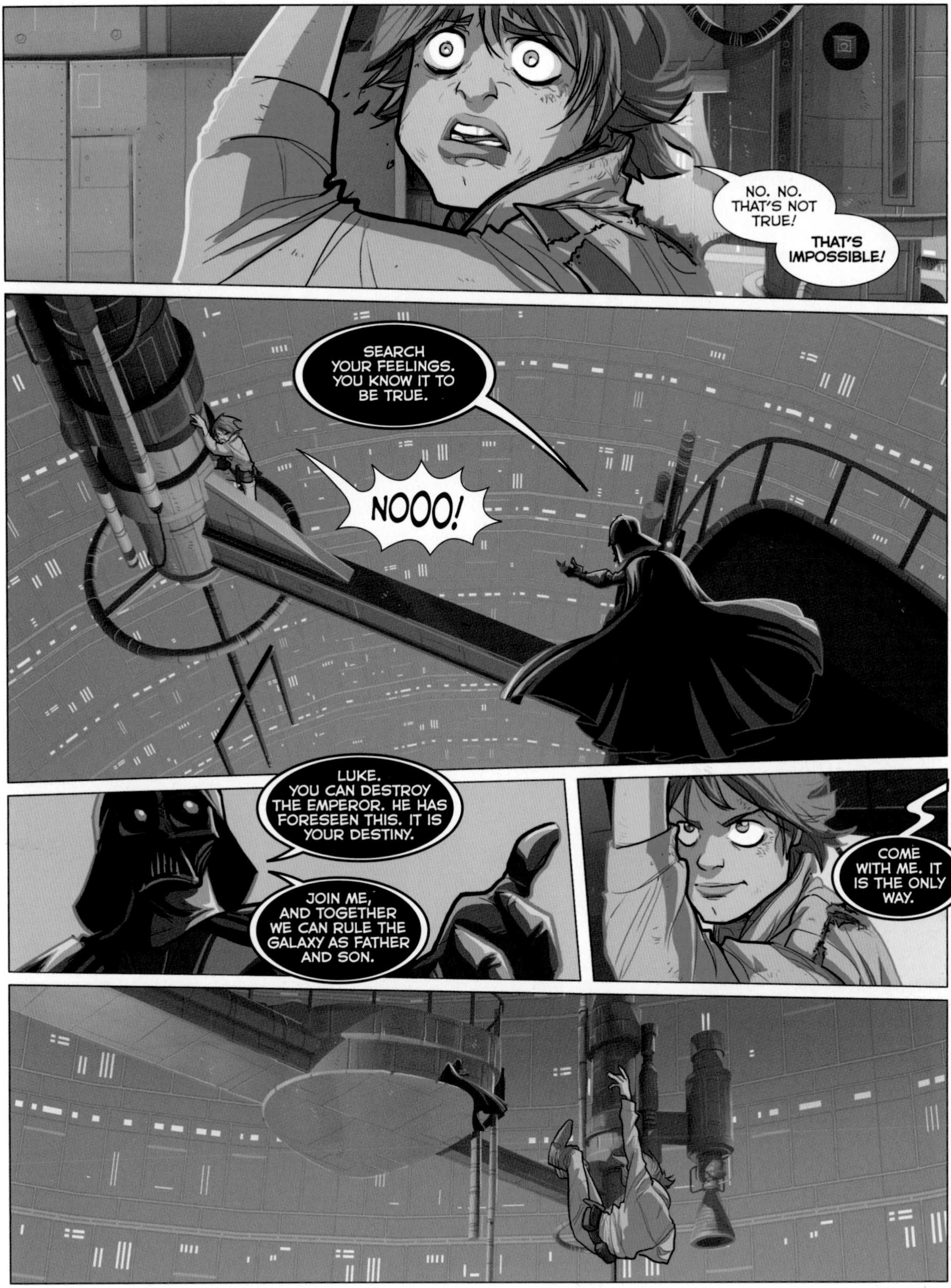
NO. NO. THAT'S NOT TRUE!
THAT'S IMPOSSIBLE!
SEARCH YOUR FEELINGS. YOU KNOW IT TO BE TRUE.
NOOO!
LUKE. YOU CAN DESTROY THE EMPEROR. HE HAS FORESEEN THIS. IT IS YOUR DESTINY.
JOIN ME, AND TOGETHER WE CAN RULE THE GALAXY AS FATHER AND SON.
COME WITH ME. IT IS THE ONLY WAY.

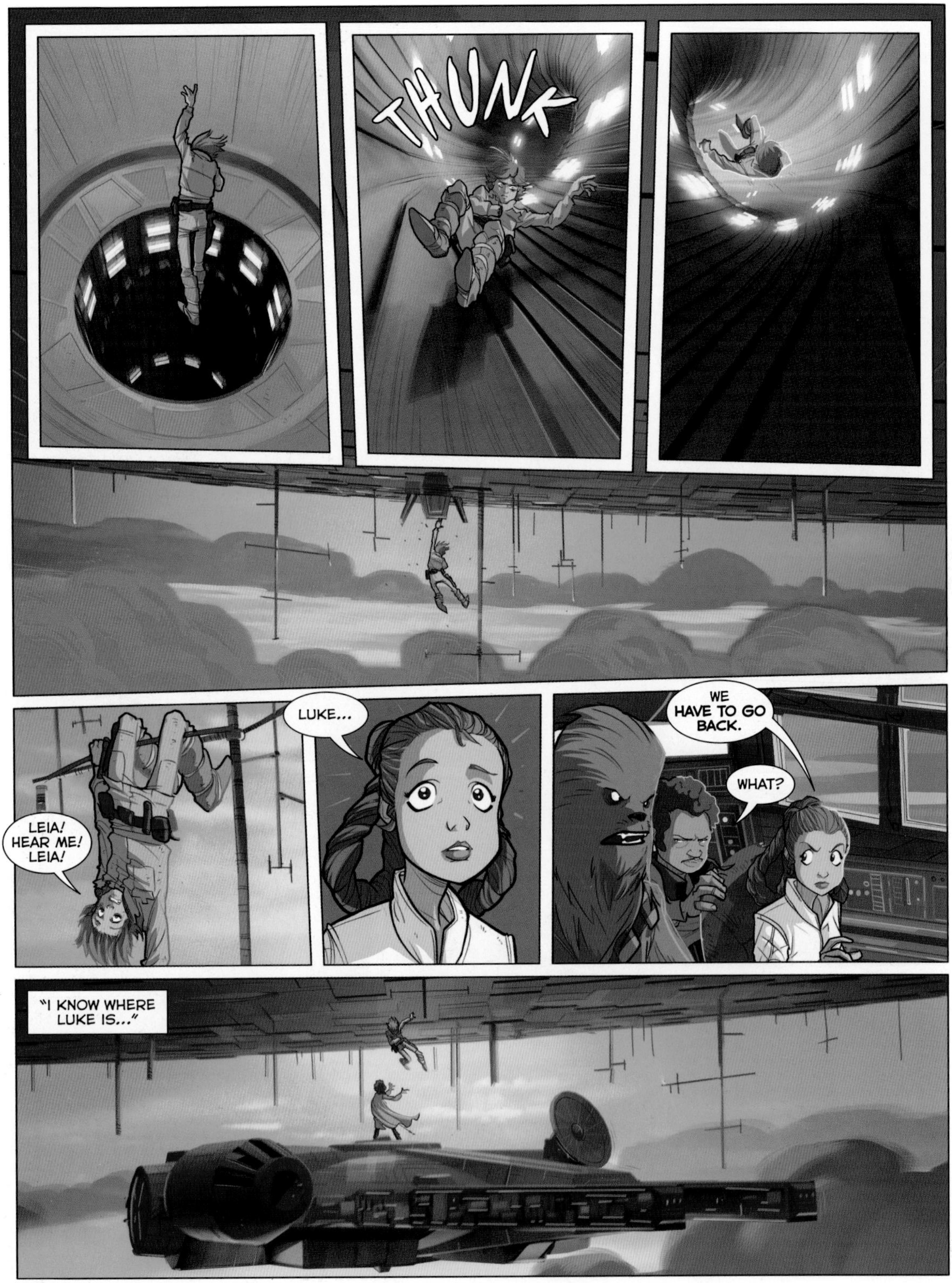
THUNK
LEIA! HEAR ME! LEIA!
LUKE...
WE HAVE TO GO BACK.
WHAT?
"I KNOW WHERE LUKE IS..."

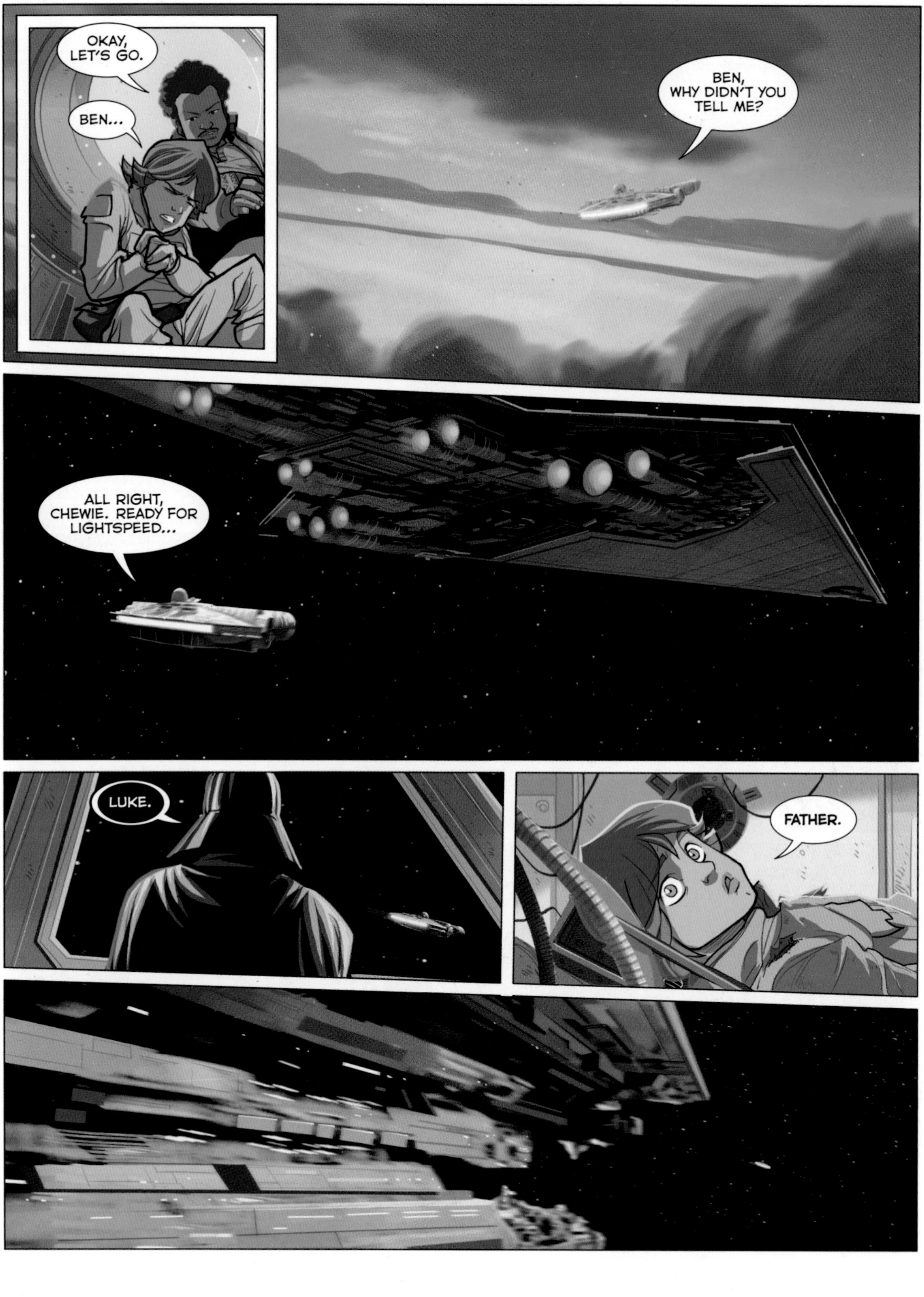
OKAY, LET'S GO.
BEN...
BEN, WHY DIDN'T YOU TELL ME?
ALL RIGHT, CHEWIE. READY FOR LIGHTSPEED...
LUKE.
FATHER.

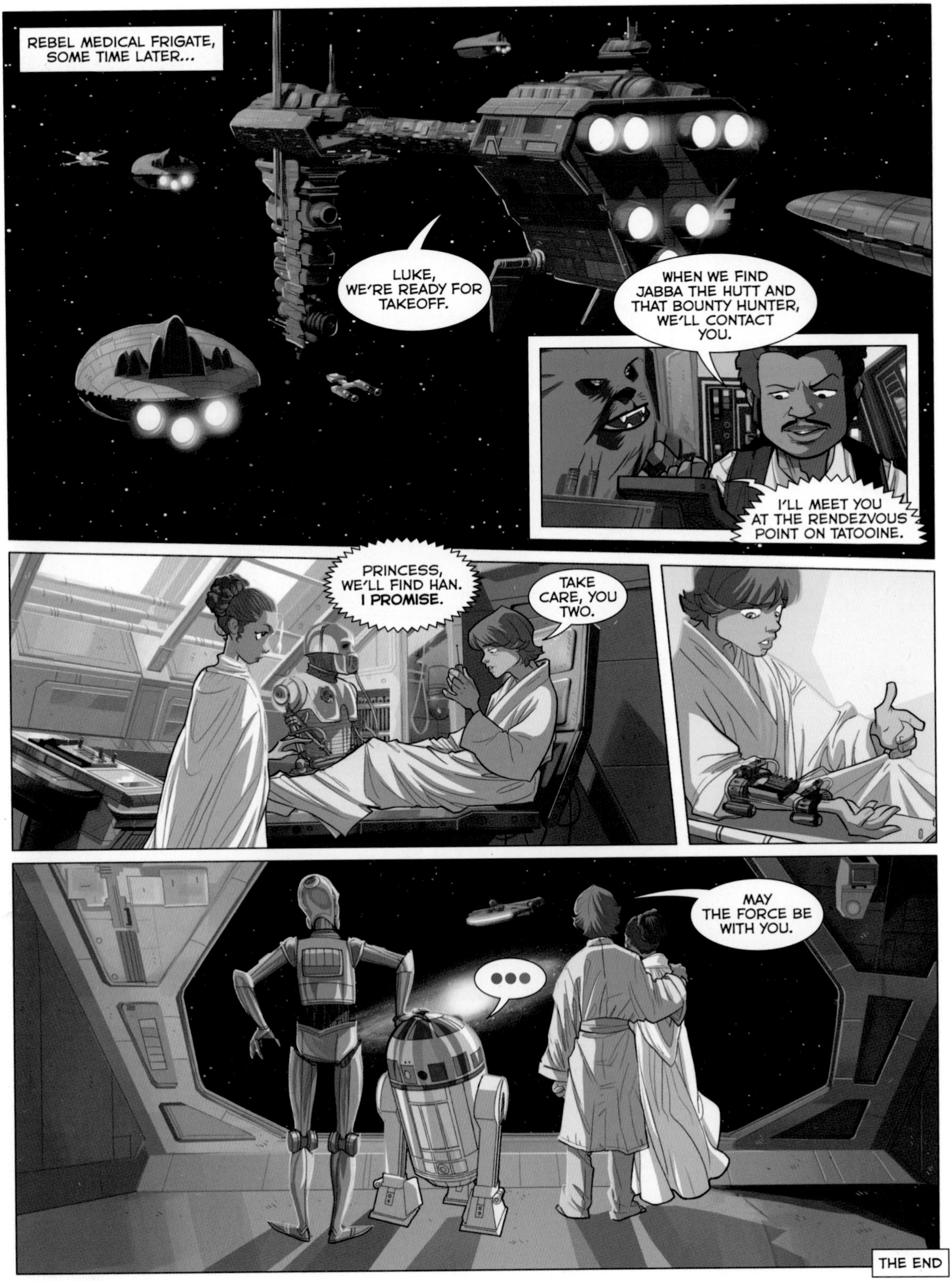
REBEL MEDICAL FRIGATE, SOME TIME LATER...
LUKE, WE'RE READY FOR TAKEOFF.
WHEN WE FIND JABBA THE HUTT AND THAT BOUNTY HUNTER, WE'LL CONTACT YOU.
I'LL MEET YOU AT THE RENDEZVOUS POINT ON TATOOINE.
PRINCESS, WE'LL FIND HAN. **I PROMISE.**
TAKE CARE, YOU TWO.
MAY THE FORCE BE WITH YOU.
•••
THE END

"TRY NOT. DO. OR DO NOT. THERE IS NO TRY."

Yoda

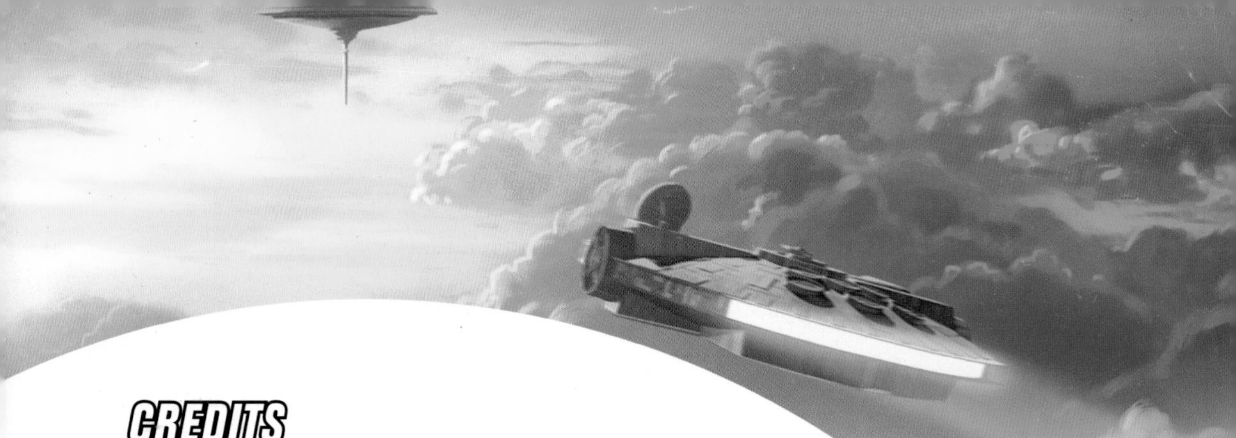

CREDITS

Manuscript Adaptation
Alessandro Ferrari
Character Studies
Igor Chimisso
Layout
Matteo Piana
Clean Up and Ink
Igor Chimisso
Paint (background and settings)
Davide Turotti
Paint (characters)
Kawaii Creative Studio
Cover
Eric Jones
Special Thanks to
Michael Siglain, Jennifer Heddle,
Rayne Roberts, Pablo Hidalgo,
Leland Chee

Based on the story by George Lucas

DISNEY PUBLISHING WORLDWIDE
Global Magazines, Comics and Partworks

Editorial Director
Bianca Coletti
Editorial Team
Guido Frazzini *(Director, Comics)*
Stefano Ambrosio *(Executive Editor, New IP)*
Carlotta Quattrocolo *(Executive Editor, Franchise)*
Camilla Vedove *(Senior Manager, Editorial Development)*
Behnoosh Khalili *(Senior Editor)*
Julie Dorris *(Senior Editor)*

Design
Enrico Soave *(Senior Designer)*
Art
Ken Shue *(VP, Global Art)*
Roberto Santillo *(Creative Director)*
Marco Ghiglione *(Creative Manager)*
Stefano Attardi *(Computer Art Designer)*
Portfolio Management
Olivia Ciancarelli *(Director)*
Business & Marketing
Mariantonietta Galla
(Marketing Manager),
Virpi Korhonen
(Editorial Manager),
Editing – Graphic Design
Absink, Edizioni BD

For IDW:
Editors
Justin Eisinger and Alonzo Simon
Collection Design
Christa Miesner
Publisher
Greg Goldstein

For international rights, contact **licensing@idwpublishing.com**

ISBN: 978-1-68405-408-4

22 21 20 19 1 2 3 4

Greg Goldstein, President & Publisher • **John Barber**, Editor-in-Chief • **Robbie Robbins**, EVP/Sr. Art Director • **Cara Morrison**, Chief Financial Officer • **Matthew Ruzicka**, Chief Accounting Officer • **Anita Frazier**, SVP of Sales and Marketing • **David Hedgecock**, Associate Publisher • **Jerry Bennington**, VP of New Product Development • **Lorelei Bunjes**, VP of Digital Services • **Justin Eisinger**, Editorial Director, Graphic Novels and Collections • **Eric Moss**, Sr. Director, Licensing & Business Development

Ted Adams, IDW Founder

www.IDWPUBLISHING.com

Facebook: **facebook.com/idwpublishing** • Twitter: **@idwpublishing** • YouTube: **youtube.com/idwpublishing**
Tumblr: **tumblr.idwpublishing.com** • Instagram: **instagram.com/idwpublishing**